TEXAS FIGHT

Book 8

AMERICA FALLS

Scott Medbury

SCOTT MEDBURY

Table of Contents

Part 1: A New Home

Part 2: Operation Underdog

Part 3: The Mole

ISBN: 9798848611281

PART 1: A NEW HOME

Chapter 1

July 7th

Jack contemplated the flat river stone in his hand. Its surface was smooth, but one side was marred by a long shallow chip, as if it had been struck by a ricocheting bullet, revealing the lighter stone inside.

He was sitting in the long grass with his legs outstretched, looking out over Grace Lake, and the endless line of trees beyond. The Sam Houston National Forest.

He pulled his hand back and launched the stone out across the wind-chopped water.

As he had nearly everyday since Grandpa had saved their bacon in his old fighter plane six months before, Jack dwelled on the memories of those he had lost. While on the run, it hadn't been so bad, but life in camp wasn't so hectic and it was easy to get caught up in regrets and grief during quiet moments.

The loss of his Mom and Dad was more about just missing them, but the others? Well, there was shame and bitterness at himself for those.

There was Danny, his best friend, who had fought by his side to rescue Katie from the psycho, Dawson, and was killed for his trouble. Whenever Jack asked himself the question about whether he could have kept him alive by doing things just a little differently, the answer was almost certainly yes.

And then there was Katie herself. The grief for his sister burnt differently, seasoned with guilt that churned in the pit of his soul, not relenting even for a day. Jack tried everything. Long walks. Helping out in the camp. Reading. Hunting. But nothing worked.

Long night watches were even worse. Staring out into the dark between the trees, he'd hallucinate Katie emerging, only to blink it away in an instant.

She'd died because of him. Had he been smarter, Katie would still be alive today, and that was an indisputable fact.

During his time in Grandpa's camp, Jack's anger and hatred of the invaders had escalated and simmered just below the surface, rising during quiet moments like this.

He picked up another stone and hurled it into the water.

'Going to war on the lake, too, huh?'

Jack turned and saw Jen strolling up to his spot on the shore, hands in her pockets.

'Are they mad I ran off?' Jack asked.

Jen shrugged.

'Not really. Grandpa figured you'd be out here.'

'Sure.'

'Not kidding,' she said, taking a place in the grass next to him. 'They're worried about you, and they get it. We've all lost family.'

'Well, your cousin Robert is still breathing, isn't he?'

Jen's face fell and he immediately apologized.

'I'm sorry Jen. That was mean and dumb. I'm a crummy friend.'

'It's okay. I know you didn't mean it, and yeah, you sure are hard work sometimes,' she said with a grin.

He grinned back.

'You'll always have Robert and me,' she said more seriously. 'But I don't just want us to be tag alongs until you shoot yourself in the head.'

Jack jerked his head around, shocked by the blunt language.

'No chance of that—'

'I know. Sorry, that was rude. But Jack, this isn't just a bad weekend. This is the occupation and we're on the run from the Chinese army—anyone who said they haven't contemplated suicide would be lying.' She put a hand on his. 'But we still have each other, right?'

'Right,' Jack sighed, stretching out his legs and rubbing his eyes. 'Sorry. Bad day.'

'Sure. You seem to have more than your fair share.'

'Gimme a break,' he said, grinning at the sly dig. 'I'm not that bad.'

Jen smirked.

'Come on, dust yourself off and walk back with me. It'll be dark by the time we get back.'

Jack and Jen got up, dusting themselves off and cast one last look over the water, inhaling the clean air and the cool approach of twilight. Jack felt much better for his interaction with Jen.

'Reckon we'll ever take it back?' he asked, shoving his hands in his pockets as they began walking.

'No,' Jen replied. 'But I think we'll survive.'

Their slow walk back to the main camp, nestled deep in the heart of the national park, took them off the conventional dirt tracks and small roads, into the trees and over ground that was littered with branches and shrubbery.

Now a solid week into the month of July, the daily temperatures were hitting close to 100F. As accustomed as he was to the heat of a Californian summer, Jack still didn't enjoy it. His t-shirt was sticking to his back just a few minutes into their walk back to camp.

A large shape darted from their left and across the path they were taking, drawing a squeal of surprise from Jen. Jack laughed in delight as the big buck sped off into the trees.

'Don't see that every day!'

'No, you don't,' said Jen, leaning against a tree. 'I need a drink.'

He wiped a forearm across his face, drenched in sweat, and pulled a small water flask from his backpack. Jen had done the same, swigging generously from her canteen.

Since arriving, Jack had seen his fair share of game. Mostly small, but this was the first time he'd seen a deer up close. According to one of the camp's hunters, a 17-year-old with distinctive blonde curly hair who went by the name of Jessie, their population was increasing. As yet Grandpa hadn't approved hunting anything larger than a rabbit for meat, something that seemed to gall Jessie no end.

Jack had a feeling they would be making a dent in that deer population as soon as their foraging teams found it harder to find canned foods. They were already casting their net wider than some of them felt safe.

'Ever get used to the heat back home?' Jack asked as they rested.

Jen shook her head.

'Robert's great with the heat, but I grew up in Michigan, originally, before moving down to be with the rest of my family. I suck. Anything over 75 kills me.'

'We escaped to the wrong damn place then.' Jack smiled. 'Maybe we need to find a rebel base somewhere north?'

'Nah, I like it here.' She screwed the top of her canteen back on and slipped it back into her backpack. 'I mean, I *really* like it here. We were lucky to find good people.'

Jack navigated a fallen branch on the forest floor as they resumed their trek.

'They are good people,' he agreed. 'But should we stick around, I mean? Is this right?'

Jen stopped and looked at him, with her eyebrows raised.

'What?' she asked.

They had both picked up the pace a half mile back and their breath was hurried.

Jack shrugged.

'I dunno, just thinking out loud, I guess. We are so close to Houston, it's dangerous and I don't see how we can stay forever. We could go north. East, maybe? You've heard the rumors about New York State. If it's true, we'd be safer there.'

'And what about the people here, huh?'

'Yeah, I don't know. Forget it, just bouncing ideas.'

He carried on walking, with Jen having to play catch up.

After another mile, they arrived at Camp Lisa, the name given to what was essentially their guerilla base, hidden miles away from open roads with the town of Huntsville to their west.

Charlie Lin, known by all as Grandpa, had helped establish the camp with a sizeable group of teenagers and other young survivors in the first month after the invasion began. His wife, Lisa, a woman of Irish descent, had died of the Pyongyang flu during Hell Week, and so in her memory, their camp had been named *Lisa*.

Amongst the cohort kicking in at an average age of 15, Charlie's only living relative, Hailey Lin, somehow spared from the flu by virtue of her shared genes, was in her early thirties and in charge of the weapons armory.

At the outer perimeter of the camp, the eldest patrolled. Grandpa had trained those over 16 in weapons and patrol tactics. If you wanted to sneak into the place, you wouldn't get far without alerting one of the guards. Further in, but still well out from the center, a small cluster of rudely constructed tents and more permanent shelters had been erected. While these housed some supplies, they were actually a booby-trapped decoy in case of an incursion from the enemy.

The real camp was 500 yards beyond these. Jack and Jen walked into the center of the camp, through supply tents to the area at the heart of their rebel base.

When Jack had first arrived, his jaw had hit the floor. Snaking between each section of tents and shelters, ran trenches as deep as six feet. It reminded him of those scenes in old war movies, with the design at Camp Lisa only lacking barbed wire and sandbags.

'We're concealed deep in the forest, but our presence has to remain undetected,' Grandpa had explained to Jack, Robert and Jen as they took their first tour of the camp back in January. 'We spent a month digging these trenches to help us navigate unseen. The supply tents close by are all built with branches and leaves, or the green canvas. Our decoy tents are under heavy foliage but will be seen first from ground level if an attack ever happens.'

Jack had found the entire set-up impressive. A real operation. Back then, it had given him comfort for the first time since his foster parents had died. It wasn't four walls, but it was a sort of home.

Only now, with his mind wandering daily to grief, he was beginning to doubt even that.

'Hey there, you with us?'

Theo, one of the survivors and third-in-command behind Grandpa and Hailey, was a tall, dark-haired kid a year older than Jack, and taller by an inch. He was popular and respected in camp and was always busy getting his hands dirty.

Jen laughed.

'He's with us. We're just tired, right Jack?'

'Right,' he said, almost grunting his response.

'Alrighty,' Theo said. 'Well, dinner is being served so you're just in time.'

'Who's cooking this round?'

On a rotating roster, every week someone new had the opportunity to cook for the camp. With a headcount of about 30, it wasn't an easy task, but with a few supporting hands, it meant everyone had their fair shot at providing and nourishing those whose sides they lived and fought by.

Jack had been reticent of the practice at first, but soon appreciated the bonding it created.

'Bradley this time,' Theo replied. 'So no more charred rabbit.'

'Thank god!' Jen smirked. 'We all love Billy, but he sure sucks ass at barbecuing meat.'

With spirits lifted, all three chuckling and

exchanging quips about the culinary capabilities of their comrades, they ventured through the trenches across the camp and then climbed up to enter the largest tent. It was a huge canvass tarpaulin, camouflaged by leaves and grasses and strung between two big oak trees.

Under the big shelter were three long tables and benches for seating, all fashioned from timber harvested by Grandpa and his survivors. They were rickety and rough but did the job. At the far end was a serving table where the food was dished out. Most in the camp were already seated when they arrived.

Grandpa was at the head of the far table and rose as Theo, Jack and Jen approached, the last to be seated. Robert, Jen's cousin, moved up to give her room, Jack taking the seat opposite Jen. Bowls of steaming stew had already been put at their places.

'Glad you could join us. Now folks, I know y'all hear me bust your asses day and night with speeches like this, but I have some good news to share.'

Jack looked up, curious.

'We're still alive!' He yelled and laughed uproariously at his dad joke.

Jack sagged in his seat, as Grandpa continued.

'God gives us the tools. We take them, we use them, and we keep fighting. He also gives us mercy, so on that note, kids, I'm about to shut my damn hole. Dig in!'

The younger survivors giggled, whilst the

attractive American-Chinese woman next to him shook her head. His daughter Hailey. The fabled armorer and the adoptive mother-figure of the group.

Dinner didn't go down as easily as Jack anticipated. His appetite was gone as old ghosts came back again to haunt him, so he offered the rest of his stew to a kid on his left called Damien. He excused himself from the table in the midst of the post-meal chatter and weaved his way out of the tent and headed back to the woods.

He didn't go far, just to a tree stump he'd sat at before, but far enough that no one would stumble across him. Suddenly, emotions overwhelmed him, and he buried his face in his hands, and cried for Katie.

Chapter 2

July 8th

The next morning, a faint, silver ray of light broke the canopy and stirred Jack awake. Stifling a yawn, he climbed up out of his bedroll and stretched, figuring the time to be somewhere on the wrong side of 6am.

Stomach growling, Jack cursed himself for not finishing his dinner, and ventured off toward the armory. Like clockwork, Hailey was already working inside the dimly lit armory tent, beginning her morning routine of weapons cleaning and inventory.

Some might call her obsessive, but Jack appreciated her attention to detail when it came to maintaining the weapons they could be called to use with a moment's notice.

Back in school, he'd been part of the shooting team and care around and for the guns had been drummed into him by his coach, Mr. Harrison. He'd also been a member of the football team, but aside from running and dodging, none of the other football skills except strategy translated to his new reality.

He cleared his throat to give Hailey the heads up on his approach as she handled one of the only Desert Eagles in their possession.

'Morning,' he yawned.

'Morning Jack. Did you sleep okay?'

Her morning voice rasped deeper than Jack had expected it to and, though he'd gotten to know Hailey quite well, it still caught him off guard occasionally as it didn't quite match her soft features.

Jack shrugged.

'Enough, I guess.'

Hailey didn't reply, dismantling the pistol into its main components on the table. To her side, she had a cloth and some oil. While he watched, she picked up a long, spindly tool that she slid inside the gun's chamber. Jack took a seat next to her, folded his arms onto the benchtop and watched silently.

After a half hour, Hailey had finished two handguns then went to work on a rifle, one of the handful they had obtained from their raids on abandoned homes over the months.

From their arsenal, Jack had been acquainted with Type 95s of varying quality. The one she started on looked like an AK47, but he was sure it wasn't.

'Type 80?' he asked.

She shook her head.

'Close.'

'Type 81?'

'Bingo,' she said.

'But it takes the same bullets as an AK47, right?' he said, trying to win back some points.

She nodded.

'So do a lot of rifles of similar build, but I'll give you the point. Good effort.'

'Nice.'

'So,' Hailey said. 'What's doing with you, kid?'

'Nothing.'

'Bullshit,' she said, and her sinewy arm flexed, jerking the gas piston free. 'Look, it's none of my business, but you've been moping for weeks now. Want to do something about it? Get busy.'

Jack knew she was right, and also knew that the less there was to do around camp, the more he thought about Katie and Hell Week and the rest of it.

'You're right. God damn it, I just wish we were doing something.'

Hailey held up the rifle.

'Er, earth to Jack. We are. What do you think we're doing holed up in the dirt? Are we making daisy chains and singing Kum-fucking-baya?'

Jack laughed and Hailey nodded as if she'd unlocked an achievement.

'Chin up, kid,' she said, when she finished putting the Type 81 back together. 'We ain't dead yet. Want to help me with the inventory before the others get up?'

'Sure thing,' he said, standing up and following her.

***

Just after 8am Grandpa was in the bushes

finishing his morning pee. He zipped up and put his hands on his lower back, arching it backward until he heard a loud pop.

'Much better,' he sighed.

Going back into the small enclosure he shared with his daughter Hailey, he slipped on his hiking boots, threw on a faded Stone Roses t-shirt and brushed his teeth with a spit of water and some old toothpaste.

Checking his features in a cracked piece of mirror, he gave himself a smile, watching the crows-feet extend and the frown lines deepen.

That's the deal, he thought. *Weary bones and wrinkles, the trade for a long life.*

Satisfied he was presentable, he ventured out of the small tent, and walked quietly past the larger dorm tents where the kids slept, to the first trench which sloped down into the earth and wound its way through toward the center of the camp like a main artery.

Navigating it at a leisurely pace, he smiled and greeted the camp's occupants as he passed. They were nearly all teenagers, which reminded him that, despite their best efforts, they weren't able to save everyone, particularly the younger ones who were mostly dead or captured in the weeks after the invasion. He could count on one hand the children in camp under the age of 10.

Instinctively, he rubbed the scar on his ribcage through the thin material of his shirt. The healed bullet wound was now a symbol of his hatred for the forces that had murdered so many and invaded his adopted home.

He reached the center of the camp, a large dugout which housed most of their equipment and goods. In the event of an attack, all survivors could fall back here to defend it. It would be where they made their last stand, if it ever came to that.

His beloved plane, Betsy, was stationed three miles away from Camp Lisa, protected from the elements and hidden under a heavy duty and well camouflaged tarpaulin to avoid discovery. She was literally 10 feet away from a paved access road that wound its way through the northwest section of the park, but unless you knew she was right there, she was almost invisible to the naked eye.

That road, which was anything but a safe runway, was where he landed her after his last mission, rescuing Jack, Robert and Jen. She'd been hidden well before the inevitable and prolonged aerial searches that followed the small victory.

Navigating the containers of food, barrels of water, and boxes of looted supplies, Grandpa ascended the nearest steps—planks of wood jammed tight into the ground to form a rudimentary ladder—and once on ground level approached the armory, where he found his daughter elbow deep in work with Jack.

'Good morning you two. How y'all doing?' he said. 'My daughter's not working you to the bone again, is she Jack?'

Hailey rolled her eyes at him. 'Why don't you

join us, Dad?'

'I'd only shoot my toes off, you know me.'

'I do. Figured I'd let you remind us why you're a liability 'round these parts.'

'Oh really?!' he cried, and elbowed Jack. 'Shots fired by my own flesh and blood, what do you think about that kid?'

The banter drew a grin from Jack, whose fingers were blackened and greased from gun oil as he wrote on the paperwork beside him. He was a good kid and a good addition to the camp.

'So,' Hailey continued, her playful banter softening a little for a serious question. 'You want me or Jack?'

'If Jack isn't too occupied, I'd like to borrow him for a minute or two.'

'Sure. We're almost done.'

Jack followed Grandpa, who headed towards the food tent.

'So, what's up?' Jack asked.

'All in good time. Let's eat first.'

***

Jack didn't surprise himself, or Grandpa, with the way he shoveled the warm oats into his mouth. Starved from not finishing last night's stew, his body craved a second helping.

Between mouthfuls, he found himself wishing they could still eat toast, or have the eggs they ate only occasionally with bacon. Unfortunately, the apocalypse didn't cater for dietary whims. Oats was the only thing they could feasibly stock to eat for breakfast. Like their rice and pasta stores it had a shelf-life of up to a year or two. In a place like Camp Lisa, more than a handful of chickens wouldn't work.

'My God,' Grandpa laughed, after he finished his second helping. 'And here I was, thinking *I* was a little peckish. All good now, son?'

Jack nodded.

'Yes sir—sorry, Grandpa.'

'It's been six months; you should know not to be so formal.'

'I know,' Jack said. 'Can't help it.'

'It's no problem. The younger kids do it, too.'

'So, what did you want to speak to me about?' Jack said, leaning his elbows onto the table and watching a group of the survivors start to collect the breakfast dishes

Outside he could see one of the oldest, Jessie, organizing a drill exercise to keep up camp fitness. Another activity that was rostered and rotated amongst the older kids.

Grandpa snapped his attention away with a cough.

'Well,' he said. 'Word has reached me, Jack, that you've not been doing so well.'

Jack ran his fingers through his hair.

'Who told you that? Jen? Robert? Was it Hailey?'

'It doesn't matter,' the old man replied, shifting on the bench to turn and face Jack. 'What matters is that we find out what's up and we make sure you're doing okay.'

Jack laughed.

'Why? We're at war. Hiding and fighting for our lives. My shit doesn't matter in the scheme of—'

'That's where you're wrong, son,' Grandpa snapped, his voice now steely. 'We need to fight not just with our hearts, but with our minds, too. If you're not firing on all cylinders, then neither are we. This ain't manning up on a football team because your broke your little toe, it's life or death. So, you spill, because I guarantee your buried feelings won't stay buried for long.

'Sorry, I—'

'I'm not finished.'

Jack clamped his jaw shut. He hadn't been admonished by Grandpa in the entire stretch of time he'd been with them.

'So, forget that 'man up and carry on' crap. Tell me what's bothering you. And if you don't want to, or can't, then let us know you've got it and I won't bother you again.'

'Really?'

'You have my word, son.'

Jack let out a breath he didn't know he was holding.

'I lost someone. Just like everyone else. But it's the way I lost her. It's... it's just been on my mind lately. But, you know, we've all lost, right? I can deal with it.'

Grandpa regarded him for a moment and Jack looked down at the rough wood of the table.

'Yes son,' Grandpa said finally. 'We've all lost someone. And we're all wired different. The loss you feel, it's real, but I need to know you'll be alright.'

'It's… listen.' Jack turned his body to face him. 'Grandpa. I get it. You need me on form. And I am. I'm just… I just need something to focus on apart from hanging around this fucking place, something to take my mind off Katie. When can we fight?'

Jack took a beat.

'Sorry for swearing.'

Grandpa shrugged.

'We will and when we do, you'll probably wish it was over. Back to you for now though. You been having nightmares too, kid?'

Jack failed to hide the shock in his eyes. How had the old man known? He never cried out or screamed. Or maybe he did, and no one had said anything?

'How did…?'

'A guess. So, I leave you with this, Jack. If you're where I think you're at, don't let it burn and take control. For now, find something to keep yourself occupied. I recommend something more physical than cleaning guns. It'll help take your mind off things and make you sleep better, trust me.'

Easing himself up from the bench, Grandpa gave him an affectionate pat on the shoulder, and headed off to the center of the camp, waving to someone as he went.

Jack remained seated, picking at a splinter at the edge of the table, grinding his teeth and wishing he hadn't confided in Jen. There was no doubt in his mind that after his early departure from dinner the night before, she had told Grandpa or Hailey of their conversation earlier in the afternoon.

Chapter 3

July 9th

Jessie's training regime since day two in the camp had battered Jack and the others. According to Theo, it had been implemented within a matter of a week of the camp being built—the whispered rumor in late night conversations was that a narrow escape at the start of the invasion had been largely down to poor cardiovascular fitness.

They decided that would change.

In the first month, Jack had struggled. In football training, he had conditioned himself to sprinting drills and weightlifting. This time, however, he needed to show endurance and pacing. The learning curve had been sharp, but his innate athleticism had saved him from too much agony.

By the second month, Jessie had them jogging in varying patterns of about five miles, to keep their location covert, and their training at a strong incline.

After Grandpa's little talk and finding out Jen had spoken to him, he needed this morning's longer training run to take his mind off things more than ever.

Six months in, he comfortably ran the courses, breaking off from the rest of the pack. It regularly earned him a rebuke from Jessie, who was cautious of unnecessary danger and risk, particularly when they had to work as a single unit to survive.

Jack's sense of reason was somewhat skewed. In the end he was just a 16-year-old kid, living in post-apocalyptic America and, like everyone else, he'd lost his country and parents, but unlike a lot of them, the guilt he carried over the death of his sister tended to cast a shadow over his mood and decisions. Sometimes he just didn't think of the greater good.

Bending down to tie the shoelaces of his Asics runners—treasures found at an abandoned Walmart outside Houston—Jack readied himself for that morning's 8am run.

Around him were six others from the camp, including Robert.

'So,' Jessie announced, stretching her long legs before tying her dark hair up in a ponytail. 'Are we ready for our 13-miler?'

There was a chorus of grunts and nods, with only Jack offering a more enthusiastic reaction, by way of a thumbs up.

'Incredible enthusiasm guys, come on. Hey, look, on the plus side, our perilous lives have given us the sort of cardio fitness our old lives never gave us.'

'I'd still kill for a Whataburger,' said Mo, a 14-year-old kid from the back of the group. Everyone laughed, even Jessie, who winked and pulled a finger gun.

'Wouldn't we all, Mo. But thanks to Grandpa's decision it's deer tonight if the hunting party gets lucky, got it? You all good?'

There were some yells of enthusiasm, including from Jack. It would be nice to have a different meat after so many months of rabbit and squirrel.

Mo had lost more weight than anyone else in the camp and had really struggled early on, but perseverance and dedication had seen him become one of the fittest.

'Yep boss! I'm ready for a PB and maybe a gold medal...'

'Oh, really?' Jessie laughed, turning to Jack. 'You about to let this freshman beat you, Jack?'

Jack shrugged. 'Why not?'

'Why not for sure,' Jessie agreed.

She made sure everyone had stretched, then checked her watch, and gave them a count before they took off south on their usual trail.

The short lap of a mile and a half around the camp meant they had to clock in a good few laps to make the 13-mile half marathon, but it was worth the overcaution to stay close to camp rather than going wider out and risk being spotted by the Chinese military in the area that they had dubbed 'Texas Command'.

Jack fell into his usual pace of nine minutes a mile. Given he had started off on over fifteen previously, he was happy with the progress. Today, though, he figured he'd play to the competition and burn some of his pent-up frustration to make it under nine minutes.

On his last outing, Jack had missed out by a hair on a sub-two-hour half marathon. Jessie had commended his fitness and encouraged him not to be discouraged since they were on a sub-optimum diet for their needs. But Jack wanted more. He needed more.

With his legs pumping in an even rhythm and feet landing directly beneath his center of mass to keep his running motion efficient, Jack soon lost himself in the blur of trees whizzing by on his left and right, accompanied by the sound of undergrowth and dry twigs crunching beneath his feet.

Even with an 8am start, the July heat would tax their hydration. By the time Jack had reached his third mile, he was already perspiring heavily and needed to take a few deep gulps from his canteen.

It had been the same last week and the week before, and Jessie had promised them a few more months of almost 100F temperature before things cooled down toward the high 70s.

A figure appeared level with Jack on the sixth mile, a grin across his long, skinny face.

'How about it, huh?' Mo panted. 'I'm still level.'

'Nice,' Jack said.

'Sure is hot.'

Jack didn't reply, focusing instead on where his feet pounded the track. A few months ago, Hailey had taken a nasty fall, twisting her ankle. Being thirty, some of the younger kids had teased her about old age, but they all knew that it could happen to any one of them.

'Phew… not even halfway yet.'

'Save your breath,' Jack said, noticing Mo had started to pant to compensate for the extra energy he was expending to talk.

'Right, sorry.'

The awkward silence lasted as long as it took Mo to slowly drop off the pace, left behind by Jack's superior fitness and longer stride.

By mile eight, Jack was alone in third place behind Jessie and Theo, who, for now at least, were the two best runners and jostling for the win.

Perfect.

By the last mile, his water bottle was empty, and he was drenched in sweat. When Jack finally crossed the finish line, he bent over double, hands on his knees, and wheezed.

A panting Jessie came over, pouring water over him.

'Well done, champ.'

'Under two hours?' Jack asked.

'You bet. And only a minute behind Theo and me. How does it feel?'

Jack went to smile but it suddenly occurred to him the effort had been hollow, and he really got nothing from it.

He half-shrugged.

'I think I'll do fine outrunning the Chinese, that's for sure.'

Jessie's eyes narrowed, trying to get a read on

him. She opened her mouth, closed it again, then finally tapped him on the arm.

'Don't forget we have target practice before dinner tonight when the hunting party get back.'

'Cool,' he said, without a hint of emotion.

***

Hailey pressed her thumbs into her eyes, rubbed them, then sat back down and knocked back a small measure of her dead husband's favorite whiskey. The swallow went down like water before it burned, and hit the well of her stomach, warming her through.

It wasn't her usual style, pulling out the drink before the stars showed themselves, but it had been a hard day.

For the sake of the kids in her and her father's care, they had to shoulder most of the responsibility of their operation without their involvement. Only Theo and Jessie had been directly involved with planning the scouting missions.

The stress of being parent, teacher, friend, medic, and more, had worn on her more than she cared to admit. Some of them had adapted to their new lives with hardly a second thought for the past. The struggle in the eyes of those who hadn't, pained her though, and recently, Jack's struggles had worried her the most.

Sure, the other kids shared similar fates, but something in Jack's mixed feelings of grief and guilt reminded her of her husband. Their quiet stoicism was similar.

Cautious of creating attachments, Hailey had resolved to hide her maternal instincts. It had been hard to do with the others, and in many cases, she'd lost that battle, but for Jack, she couldn't. She felt that if she gave in and fully shared in his pain, it would become hers too, and pull up memories of her old life.

It would hurt too much.

As selfish as that resolution was, it all came down to preservation.

Knocking back another shot, she hid the bottle and cup under her things in the tent, grabbed the duffel bag of guns and ammo, and walked out of the camp towards the shooting range.

Located a short walk away and calculated to be the furthest from any minor roads, it meant that they could let loose with handguns and rifles, without anyone ever hearing a thing.

As an additional precaution, all firing would be done simultaneously, rather than in turns, to reduce the time spent at the range, and allow everyone to get their shooting in.

In a small clearing ahead, huddled in front of a small wooden shelter that ran long and narrow, the running group from the morning, headed by Jessie, waited patiently for her to arrive.

'Alright, you little soldiers, let's get our reps in. Today, we're going with the QSZ-92, with 9mm rounds as sadly, that's the most we have. Then it will be turns on the AR15, and their standard-issue assault rifles, the Type 81. Remind me again, why we stick primarily with Chinese weapons?'

In a droning chorus, as if repeated a million times, the group grumbled, 'To ensure we are competent with any weapon we find at our disposal.'

'Correct.'

On a table before the shooting gallery structure, all guns were lined out, with their magazines to the side and empty. As part of their practice, everyone would have to load their own magazines and weapons.

Over the months, Hailey had guided and watched as each kid went through their drills, improving every week.

She was particularly proud of the group project back in February. For a solid week, the original founders of Camp Lisa had used old fence posts and boards to construct Chinese military targets and fake environments to shoot at. It was rudimentary, but it worked.

Once everyone had finished, the air was rich with the smell of cordite, and Hailey watched as the students, keeping their weapons aimed down into a long sand box—another genius addition to the shooting gallery—removed the magazines and placed them back on the table.

Hailey was happy and heaped praise where due in spite of her mood earlier that morning.

She caught sight of Jack placing his Type 81 down with a little less care than she would have liked, and folded her arms. The kid looked happier when he was busy shooting guns, running and working on camp structures, and had been in his best moods on the few looting trips he'd made since joining, but his attitude had taken a nosedive over the last two weeks.

'Right,' Hailey announced. 'Good work. Theo, you need to keep that posture up and the aim will come. Jessie, perfect. Jack, great, but treat the guns with more care.'

She received nods and grunts in return. It looked like everyone's minds were on dinner. She didn't blame them. Hers was, too. On the menu today, was Grandpa's famous venison burgers— the hunting party had taken down a small deer.

'Let's head back for eats,' she called out after a few more minutes of shooting.

She watched Jack walk on ahead, slouching with his hands stuffed into his pockets, the high of the shooting practice clearly gone already.

Jesus, she thought, keeping a close eye on him. *He'll enjoy the looting run tomorrow, but he really needs something more. It might be time to announce to camp what we've been planning.*

Chapter 4

July 10th

Jack had been impressed with just how many camping areas populated the Sam Houston National Park. So far, according to Grandpa, they'd not needed to loot outside the park since they'd set up camp, except for one troubled run to the outskirts of Huntsville.

Aching from his run the morning before, he climbed out of his bedroll early morning, looking forward to joining in the bimonthly loot run. Out on the muddy ground, Jack extended his legs one at a time, reaching down to touch his toes, stretching his hamstrings.

After a few more of the moves Jessie had taught him, he felt limber enough to tackle the day.

Coming out of their tent, Robert gave Jack a wave. Unlike him and Jen, once the three fugitives had been rescued and began living amongst other people, Jack and Robert had become a little distant.

Fleeing for their lives had brought them together, but as people the two were not particularly compatible. Still, they were on good terms, but more like roommates with a shared experience, than friends.

'Morning,' he said. 'How good were those burgers?'

'Pretty dang good!'

'Ready for the mission?'

'Sure. You?'

Robert joined Jack on the walk around the outside of the camp, to the planning area. Jack rubbed sleep from the corner of his eyes and pushed his hair back from his brow. It was about time to ask Hailey for a haircut. Having seen some of her handiwork, he had been putting it off as long as he could. He'd heard a few people say she was improving, but he'd seen one too many *Dumb and Dumber* fringes to have any confidence.

Robert had a big smile on his face when he saw where they would be patrolling.

'What?' Jack asked. 'Are you in the market for a widescreen TV?'

Robert laughed and shook his head.

'You know Murphy?'

Jack frowned, then clicked his fingers.

'Um, quiet black girl? The one who saved Todd from drowning back in the spring?'

'The very same.'

'Oh, you like her? You're not looking to find her a gift, are you?'

Robert looked offended.

'Why not? Look, she told me she loves jewelry. So, I thought, what better place to loot for them than in the bigger accommodation units on the south edge of the park, right?'

Jack shrugged.

'So, she likes you back?'

Robert's face reddened.

'I think so. I mean, maybe? I won't know unless I try, right?'

'Why not just talk to her?'

'What?' Robert dropped his voice as they edged closer to the planning tent, surrounded by more of their fellow survivors. 'Dude, I need a fallback. She wouldn't talk to me otherwise—I'm friggin' weird.'

'Who said you're weird?'

'Jen.'

Jack laughed for the first time in what felt like days. It felt odd.

'Of course she's gonna say that Robert. She's family. Actually though,' he added. 'You are a tiny bit weird, but not enough to make it a problem with the opposite sex.'

Robert thumped him in the arm and they both chuckled.

Energized and eager for the mission, Jack approached the planning table and waited for Hailey to finish spreading the map out. Opposite Jack, next to Hailey, stood Theo, towering over them all. Next to Theo, much to Robert's chagrin, was Murphy, who was laughing at something Theo had said. Jack could practically feel the jealously radiate from Robert.

Hailey clapped her hands together to silence everyone.

'So, campers, it's me in charge again, and we'll be a team of five instead of four,' she announced loudly and jabbed her finger at the map. 'This will be our target.'

Jack, Robert, Murphy and Theo all leaned over to inspect the area of the map she highlighted. It was an area south of their position, clustered on the west side of Lake Livingston.

Theo whistled.

'Cape Royale? We sure that's a good idea?'

Hailey narrowed her eyes at him.

'Sorry,' he said.

'Don't apologize, Theo,' she said, her face softening. 'It's a good question. Why are we hitting Cape Royale? Why the risk?' She straightened her back, folded her arms and looked each one of them in the eye.

'Grandpa and I are planning something big. Some of you know about it, but we're keeping it under wraps until we feel it's time to divulge it to the whole camp. I know, it's all a bit cloak-and-dagger, but we have a few details we need to hammer out. That being said, we're going to need supplies. Lots of supplies, so we need to hit a bigger cache if we want to implement our plans.'

'Is this anything to do with the rumors about a guerilla attack?' Murphy asked.

Hailey smirked, shaking her head.

'You guys don't miss a trick, huh?'

Robert and Theo shook their heads, and it was Jack, now, who felt the idiot. Apparently, he'd been so caught up in his own issues, that he'd been completely ignorant to the talk around him.

Hailey saw his frown.

'I guess not everyone. But that's fine. We were all going to find out sooner or later. Tonight will be as good a time as any.'

'What is it?'

'We call it Operation Underdog.'

An uncomfortable tension started to manifest in the tent, not least from Robert, who even though he hadn't deliberately kept it from Jack, couldn't help but feel guilty for not keeping him in the loop.

'Operation Underdog will be a stealth operation against the new Chinese Fuel Facility, the main aim to destroy all fuel containers.'

They all stared at Hailey with slack jaws. Even the ones like Theo who had heard the rumors weren't aware of the ambition of the operation. He had figured it would be something big, but the plan still hit him in the gut.

Jack was impressed at the scale of it. The opportunity. The risk.

'It's about time we fought back!' said Jack, smiling like he'd just won the lottery.

Hailey held up a hand.

'Easy, bucko, this isn't the time to be gunslinger. It'll be a covert, highly dangerous mission, and if all goes to plan, we won't need to fire a single shot. We want to cripple the facility and ruin their logistical operations in Texas. It may also give us further opportunities, but Grandpa will no doubt cover those tonight.'

'Jeez,' Theo breathed.

'Yeah,' Robert said, scratching his head. 'That's friggin' major. Do er… do you know who's going on the mission?'

Everyone turned to Hailey, completely forgetting the map and their looting plans.

'No,' she said. 'That's still being worked out.' She checked her watch and clapped her hands again. 'For now, get your heads back in the game at hand: our run to Cape Royale!'

Over the methodical thud of the team's boots, and the rustle of wind in the leaves above, hearty chatter occupied their trek southeast to Cape Royale.

Despite the pep talk Hailey had given them before they set out, a sense of unease stirred underneath the bravado and quiet laughter. News of the operation that might bring extra attention on them was an ominous sign that things might soon get far more perilous for the camp.

By noon, they were soaked through from the heat again and had covered miles of ground, passing vacation homes they'd already raided over the last few months.

Shaded by the trees, they stopped at about one o'clock to eat some nuts and tinned peaches washed down with filtered water. They were in sight of Cape Royale by 3pm.

It had been a sprawling community, with plenty of open and wooded spaces between residences. Hailey decided to split them into two groups and to Jack's surprise, she paired him with Theo, while she paired with Murphy and Robert.

Not so bothered by the choice, Jack led the way once the groups had separated.

Theo, even with his longer stride, had to motor to keep up.

'You seem keen for the mission to the fuel facility, Jack. Are you looking for action, or just wanting to stick it to the Chinese?'

'Why not both?' Jack retorted, peering in through the front windows of a big double-story home to check for corpses.

The one thing they all hated finding was the dead. People who had died slumped in their chairs or beds. Given the infection had been in winter, a lot of the buildings they'd searched before had been vacant, but once you'd had the misfortune to encounter a dead homeowner, it was enough to make you wary whenever you crossed a threshold.

'All clear?' Theo asked.

'As far as I can see. Let's have look.'

Balancing on his left foot, Jack kicked his right foot into the door just below the handle. It took two more kicks before the door buckled inwards. It bounced off the wall, and Jack neatly dodged it, sweeping his pistol left and right as he stepped inside.

Hailey never let them loot unarmed.

Jack could hear Theo right behind him, padding as quietly as Jack, his breath steady and measured.

Within a minute, they had cleared both floors,

and the area out back. No dead bodies. No lurking Chinese soldiers.

'Clear,' Jack shouted from upstairs.

'Clear,' Theo responded from outside.

They went about emptying the drawers, and anything under the beds. They found nothing useful like weapons or tools apart from some matches and two fresh packs of AA batteries, but the cupboards in the kitchen yielded a fresh supply of canned goods.

'Jackpot,' Theo laughed. 'More peaches.' He held up a can to show Jack, adding it to his bag.

'Eh, I think I've outgrown my love for 'em if I'm being real with you.'

'Really?' Theo said. 'I still love them.'

They were silent as they finished stuffing one of the bags they were carrying.

'Well, that's this place. Might as well move on to the next.'

Before the sun started to dip in the sky, Jack and Theo had raided four houses on the south edge of Cape Royale and in addition to the batteries and matches from the first house, their bags were heavy with a few good knives, some medical supplies, sanitary products and a pair of socks along with more canned goods.

They reconvened at the lake at the allotted time, and only had to wait a few minutes for Hailey and the others to arrive.

'Great haul you guys,' Hailey said, after looking over their findings. 'We found a place to bed down for the night a quarter mile east, let's get there before we completely lose the light.'

They arrived at the abandoned home, sweaty, tired, and hungry, and threw down their bags and gear in the living room. Their chatter and laughter echoed through the house as they took turns using the toilet, an unfamiliar luxury. Robert volunteered to go down to the lake with a bucket so they could flush it.

Once the sun was down, they ate a light meal of cold canned beans and peas. Not the most thrilling of meals, but it was always a cold meal on a looting trip, more so now they were out of the confines of the national park.

After the meal, they huddled into their sleeping bags.

Jack spied Murphy looking at Robert, but he was preoccupied with his sleeping bag zip, and didn't notice.

You'll have to be more aware than that buddy, he thought.

By the time Robert was satisfied with his sleeping bag, Murphy had rolled over.

'Okay we leave at first light,' Hailey said. 'Never in darkness.'

'Never in darkness,' they intoned before saying their goodnights.

Chapter 5

July 11th

At the crack of dawn, Hailey woke them all up. With his sleeping bag around his shoulders, Jack walked out to where she stood on the balcony overlooking the lake.

A light breeze rolled up from the water, just enough to tickle the skin of his face. They watched as in silence as a large flock of a small bird he couldn't put a name to, swirled in random patterns over the lake. The sun crested through the trees to the east. Jack was struck by the beauty of the place.

'Must have been a nice spot.'

Hailey nodded.

'Still is, Jack. Just that there's no one around to enjoy it anymore.'

Within 20 minutes they had eaten breakfast and packed up ready to go, and Hailey was doing a final sweep of the house to make sure they'd left no sign of their brief occupancy. Jack checked his watch. It was just after 6am, which meant they should make Camp Lisa by lunch.

'I nearly forgot! It's Grandpa's birthday!' said Murphy, as they were heading off the verandah.

Jack turned to catch Hailey grinning broadly.

'Sure is. Anyone wanna take a guess at how old?'

Theo scrunched up his face.

'I figure... mid-sixties?'

Hailey shook her head.

'Late-sixties? Maybe 67? 68?' Robert guessed, chewing on his bottom lip.

Hailey laughed.

'Way off. Try another decade.'

They all looked at each other, jaws dropping.

'No freaking way,' Murphy said. 'So, what, is he 80?'

'Yup,' Hailey congratulated. 'Hits the big 8-0 today. Not doing too bad, right?'

'I hope I look as good if I survive to 80,' said Jack.

A silence dropped over them after that. No one spoke the thought, but living in the After Days, the chances of any of them living to 80 felt like fantasy at best.

Not far into their trek home, someone mentioned an idea for a birthday surprise and the somber mood lifted as they all took turns tossing around ideas.

The return leg was a simple case of following their previous tracks, with the back marker, in this case Theo, tasked with obscuring their tracks as they went. It was really just to make things a little more difficult in the event someone tried to track them, and if they had dogs, it was probably ineffectual but might slow them down a little.

Sweating, with aching feet and bellies rumbling for food, they practically collapsed back into camp. After dumping their loot, Hailey and Theo debriefed with Grandpa and Jessie, while the rest were dismissed to go clean up and eat.

Grandpa got lots of sweaty birthday hugs and pats on the back as they filed out of the command tent.

With a cloth, a small towel and some soap, Jack was first to the camp wash and took a little time for himself in the walled off "bathroom".

By the end of the first month in Camp Lisa, he'd grown used to water rationing and washing in cold water. Hot showers were just a distant and fond memory of the life he'd lost back in Sacramento. By month number six he couldn't begin to conceive of wasting as much water on a single wash as they had back then.

How times had changed.

After he finished getting changed into clean clothes, he checked the small mirror someone had left on the ledge beside the basin. It had been months since he'd looked in a mirror and the hard, tanned face staring back at him was almost unrecognizable. It spooked him, and he threw it down before packing his gear and heading out.

The haul from Cape Royal had been carefully organized, shoved into containers and recorded according to guidelines written up by Hailey. The canned food was ample, filling two large containers.

'We'll have to make a run for one of the towns nearby for clothes one of these days,' Jessie muttered to Jack, as he stood on a ladder hanging up decorations on a tree for Grandpa's birthday celebrations.

'Really?' he replied, looking down to where she was poking a finger through a hole in the belly of her t-shirt. The ladder wobbled and he gripped the top hard. 'Jessie!'

She laughed and steadied the ladder.

'My bad. But sure, I mean, these looting runs have done us well for food, but not so much for anything else. We need to hit a town.'

'Why haven't we gone back to Huntsville? You guys swarmed in to save us easy enough.'

Jack saw Jessie shrug in his periphery.

'Huntsville was a huge risk, but we hadn't seen survivors in ages. Houston was secured and locked down by the Chinese really quickly, so you guys were definitely the exception. Grandpa had insisted, but Hailey wasn't happy about it.'

'That I can believe.'

'Mhmm.'

'So, too dangerous?'

'Oh, for sure. They'll be keeping tabs on Huntsville and any town close by. To be honest, I'm surprised they haven't come after us here. I'm pretty sure they would know we're somewhere in the forest. I mean, why not just burn the whole thing down?'

'Don't wish that on us!' Jack said. 'I guess the trouble we caused that night was just a blip on their radar. Probably way too busy occupying a whole continent to worry about a few kids in the forest. Of course, that might change once we hit their fuel facility.'

Jessie nodded.

'Oh, you heard? Yes, things will heat up then for sure, I think. You don't like the idea?'

'I love the idea…'

'Are you guys nearly done?' asked Robert, joining them.

'Yep,' said Jessie, taking her hand off the ladder to sweep some hair out of her eyes. The ladder wobbled again, and because Jack was reaching out to the right, began to topple.

Jack jumped free, cursing as he landed on his feet and watched the ladder fall into the bushes.

'You're fired!' he said to Jessie, a grin on his face.

Grandpa's birthday celebration saw the camp imbued with a high energy, fun atmosphere none of them had experienced since before the fall. The decorations, the best and rarest of their food stash cooked and laid out onto tables, and Murphy playing music for everyone on an acoustic guitar, all added to it.

They were all in the mess tent, but tables had been put at one end and the chairs and benches laid out around the outside. The assortment of food was impressive. Spit-roasted venison, mash potato, baked beans, fresh carrots and tomatoes, and a huge batch of mac n cheese.

'Full bellies and no leftovers!' Grandpa had shouted as they filed in.

Accordingly, no one held back, plates were piled high, and seconds and sometimes thirds were the order of the day.

Jack took a seat next to Jen and Robert, laughing as Grandpa tried to dance to the shaky rendition of *Proud Mary* that Murphy was strumming. Shaky it might have been, but it was enough to get toes tapping and hands clapping.

When the song was over, there was a raucous round of applause for Grandpa and Murphy, and the old man limped over to "Chair Rock" holding his lower back.

The big rock that sat in the eastern corner of the mess tent had been way too big to dig out or move when they had set up camp. Grandpa had decided it was a good analogy for the stubbornness of their will to survive and should stay right there. It stood about five feet high and had a flattened top with a small lip on its back edge, so it had been named *Chair Rock*, although Jack hadn't seen anyone sit on it besides Grandpa, so he figured it was more like a throne.

Jack suspected Grandpa's limp and nursing his back was for show and to get out of more dancing rather than an actual injury, and sure enough, less than a minute after he sat down, the old man was up and heading for the food as spritely as he ever was.

'Feels like forever since I had mac n cheese,' Jack said, barely intelligible through large mouthfuls, waving his fork at Jen and Robert. 'Was it always this good?'

'Hell yeah,' Robert nodded.

Jen turned up her nose.

'Really? I mean, come on guys, this lot is from a can. It was never *that* great.'

Jack and Robert looked at Jen with eyebrows raised.

'She's lost to us,' Robert whispered.

'Utterly,' Jack agreed.

Jen smirked and offered them a small shrug, before finishing off her carrots.

'I'm right and you know it.'

On cue, Theo from a few seats over, closer to Grandpa, raised his empty plate up in the air and yelled his undying love for mac n cheese.

'Not according to Jen!' called Robert.

'No Jen, say it ain't so!' said Theo before resuming his seat.

Jen turned bright red, which made Robert laugh. Jack nudged him to tone it down. Clearly her reaction had something to do with her maybe crushing a little on Theo.

'Wanna give mac n cheese another go?' Robert said, not quite ready to leave it alone. The teasing earned him a solid punch to the arm from his cousin.

Leaving them to mock squabble, Jack took the opportunity to sneak back to the table and load up on some more baked beans. He dipped a ladle into the pot, and then watched them pour slowly down onto the tin plate.

Next to him, Grandpa cleared his throat loudly. Jack startled, sending some of the beans splattering into the dirt.

'Shit!'

Grandpa laughed.

'Steady on there son,' he said. 'You enjoying the party?'

Jack laughed and put the ladle back in the big pot.

'Shouldn't I be asking you that?'

'You might.'

'So... er... are you?'

Grandpa beamed.

'It's perfect. Makes the struggle worth it, kid. Seeing all your faces bright and alive. Your souls on fire, hungry for life. It keeps me going.'

'Cool. I didn't know it mattered that much. I mean, we just pitched in and stuck up some decorations—'

'Well, you all did a great job, and I'm thankful,' Grandpa interrupted, his face suddenly serious. 'Come on, leave the beans. I've an announcement to make and I'll think you'll be interested, come.'

Grandpa waved him back to his seat and went over to Chair Rock, nimbly climbing it and turning around to face everyone.

Only a few people noticed, and he raised his hands for silence.

'Speech!' one of the kids shouted in a mock British accent, getting a few laughs, and slowly everyone turned their attention to Grandpa whose eyes twinkled in the twilight.

'I want to thank you for making my birthday special. I'm happy to see my eightieth out here with the best bunch of kids I've ever had the misfortune to meet!' There were laughs and mock calls of boo. 'Now, I have a surprise for you. We were going to announce this later, but I suppose now's a good enough time as many, so, to hell with it.'

Jack saw Hailey give him an encouraging nod from the edge.

'In seven days,' said Grandpa. 'We will commence Operation Underdog, our first real offensive against the invaders. A select group of you will infiltrate the new Chinese fuel facility. The aim will be to destroy their reserves and get the hell out before they can fire a shot in anger. In seven days, we take the fight to them. It'll be dangerous and might bring them down on our heads,' he looked Jack in the eye. 'But in seven days, we finally get to kick some ass.'

Silence fell over those assembled as they contemplated the news.

'So, it's finally happening?' Jessie said.

'It sure is,' said Hailey. 'And it's about time, too.'

Chapter 6

Jack fed himself a little too well at the party. It was only thanks to a miracle haul of canned goods the day before that they got to eat so much, and the dark truth behind the abundance wasn't lost on Jack though.

Despite the cheer and optimism generated by the celebrations and the news about the coming operation, in the cold light of morning he couldn't help but figure, maybe, just maybe, the odds of them surviving were so bleak, that they didn't really need to ration the food as strictly...

Maybe they should just enjoy it while they could?

The mood in the camp had changed since Grandpa's stirring announcement. Some looked excited, others seemed trepidatious.

Robert, who had slept in a bedroll just six feet from him since they'd arrived back in the winter, looked troubled. Jen was the opposite—her bubbly conversation was met with grunts by her cousin and, when he and Jack left to start working on inventory, his mind clearly wasn't as focused as it usually was.

When Murphy had turned up to pitch in, like Jen, her entire demeanor juxtaposed Robert's. She didn't seem to notice his morose mood and surprised Jack with her energy. An hour into their chore there was not a bead of summer sweat on her, and she'd done twice the work Robert had done.

'What do you think about the mission?' Murphy asked Jack when Robert went for a bathroom break. 'I don't think Robert's a big fan.'

'Yeah, he and Jen went through some stuff before we met up. It was pretty bad, so I don't think he's too much of a fan of conflict.'

How do I feel about it? He thought.

He supposed the closest word he could use to describe it was controlled excitement. The kind of excitement he used to feel before a big game.

'I say it's about time, though.'

After noon, when the heat really started to kick everyone's ass, he decided his drifting mind wasn't much use for work that required an eye for detail, so he wandered over to Hailey's area of the camp to see what needed to be done in preparation for Operation Underdog.

Suddenly nervous, Jack lingered about outside the tent opening, fidgeting with the fabric, before Hailey called him in. She was sitting on a foldable metal chair and was looking over her glasses as she inspected the ammunition cache.

'Spit it out if you're gonna.'

Jack coughed.

'Sorry. I just didn't feel up for inventory. Head isn't er… in the right place.'

Hailey turned in her chair and raised an

eyebrow.

'Really, kid?'

Jack shrugged. 'Yeah.'

'Alright,' she said, standing up and walking toward him, forcing Jack to step back and let her out into the open air, where she walked a few paces before turning to face him, arms folded. 'Let's tackle this head-on.'

'I just need a bit of a break, like a walk or something,' Jack asked.

'Well, you know Camp Lisa isn't a holiday resort, right? It sucks you're all in this at such a young age. I get it, but we have to pull our weight.'

'I have been.'

'True,' Hailey admitted, tilting her head. 'But your head's not been in it lately. What's changed?'

'Nothing's changed,' he said, which was mostly true. 'I just…'

'Look, kid, you need to talk about what's eating you up inside.'

'Why does everyone keep saying that?'

'Because you're not facing it. You're ignoring it. Be smarter about this and trust me.'

Jack shook his head. 'I am being smart. This isn't easy.'

'You're not being smart,' Hailey reinforced, stepping closer and pointing. 'You're one of the most mature kids here, but you're bottling it up. You know you need to talk, and you know people are here to listen.'

'Whatever!' he snapped. 'I just came here to get

another—'

'Hey!'

Hailey opened out her hands, palms up, in indignation. She was shocked by Jack's rudeness.

'What?'

'Don't talk to me like that.'

Jack rubbed his eyes, and looked around, and for a moment considered just leaving. He didn't.

'Sorry,' he finally said.

Hailey let out a breath and combed her fingers through her long black hair.

'It's okay, I'm sorry too, I pushed too hard. I'm feeling it too, you know? Look. We're rotating tomorrow for key tasks. We've got two new bodies on inventory... do the others have it covered for this afternoon?'

'I think so,' said Jack. 'Murphy was like the Flash this morning.'

'Okay then. Have your break or walk or whatever. Just don't go out far, and not for too long. Okay?'

'Okay, thanks.'

Jack could feel her eyes on him as he left, taking the trenches back through the center of the camp. He grabbed his small backpack, a flask of water and put his knife in his boot before heading out.

Overhead, under the beating sun, the deep blue sky foretold nothing of the danger they would all face in seven days.

Time melted away into the heat, and Jack was

soon within sight of Grace Lake, the calm waters glinting and winking between the trees that soon gave way to a long expanse of overgrown grass.

Jack climbed onto one of the timber picnic tables that was slowly being taken over with grass. The forest would encroach on the picnic area in a few short years and soon wipe out any evidence that it had ever existed. He slipped off the small backpack, pulled out his canteen then sat cross-legged so he could rest and drink his water as he looked at the lake.

Unlike last time he was there, no one disturbed him, and he enjoyed the solace.

Minutes turned into an hour, and an hour into two. Jack watched the sun begin to dip and knew he should return before Hailey decided to send out a search party.

He eased himself off the table, threw on his backpack, and made his way back toward the camp.

He'd made it just a few minutes back along the same track when he heard movement off to his right, from a fair distance.

With his heart beating hard, he dropped down into a crouch and moved behind a tree, searching for signs of movement.

The snap of twigs echoed again. He held his breath. Waited.

Then, far off, perhaps 150 feet, Jack spotted a slim figure. He squinted, he couldn't make out much but it was close enough to determine the person was not wearing a uniform and didn't appear to be armed.

Jack scratched his head, easing himself up and staying crouched as he followed them. He soon realized they were heading in the same direction he had been traveling.

Was it someone from camp? What were they doing all the way out here? Should he call out?

Licking his lips, Jack decided to get closer to figure out who it was. He broke into a careful jog, keeping low and moving as silently as possible.

Then he recognized the mysterious figure. It was Todd from Camp.

Cupping his hands around his mouth, not really taking time to consider the risk, Jack shouted to the kid.

'Todd!'

The slim teenager spun around, hands up, eyes wide. The comical effect caught Jack off guard, and he laughed.

'Figured I was a Chinese soldier, huh?' Jack said as he jogged up to the other kid. The kid was red-faced and looked a little shaken, but he fist-bumped Jack when it was offered, looking around furtively. 'Hey, relax man, it's just me.'

'Yeah,' he breathed. 'I know. Dude… you scared the shit outta me.'

'I can see that. What were you doing all the way out here?'

Jack hadn't forgotten Todd was one of their youngest survivors at 14. As such, Hailey hadn't tasked him with any looting, scouting or guard duties. Which only made his presence so far outside of Camp Lisa that much stranger. After a pause, the kid answered.

'Just er... walking.'

'Walking? We're like an hour out.'

Todd seemed to search for words, then looked up at Jack with big brown eyes.

'Why're you all the way out here then?'

'I need a breather. Hailey gave me the nod. Does she know you're all the way out here, though?'

'Yeah. She said it was cool...' Todd said, his eyes carefully avoiding Jack's.

'Bro, seriously?'

Todd groaned, shifting his weight.

'Don't tell her, alright? She'll friggin' kill me.'

'Not my problem, dude.'

'Please, Jack. Come on.'

'So what were you doing out here then?'

Jack searched the trees from the direction Todd had come, expecting to see some small clue to his motives for unauthorized adventure, but saw none. The kid was keeping quiet.

'I...' he bowed his head, hiding his face from Jack. 'I went to speak to my Mom.'

Jack frowned. 'What?'

'My Mom. I... I go to speak to her.'

It struck him, then, what Todd had meant. A deep well of guilt churned in his gut like hot acid, and he was ashamed to feel a lump rise up in his throat. Coughing, he turned away so Todd wouldn't see him lose his shit.

'Come on,' he said, clapping the kid on the shoulder. 'I won't tell Hailey a thing. We all need a little me time now and then, right?'

'You won't?'

Jack nodded.

'Promise, it's our secret, but maybe next time tell her. She gets it.'

On the walk back, Jack talked with Todd about life before the Pyongyang virus and the invasion. Truth was, he didn't want to delve too much into the kid's personal life by drudging up memories of his parents and family. Last thing he wanted was the kid crying or anything, so he steered the conversation to things like Xbox, PlayStation, NFL and pizza.

In contrast to his walk to Grace Lake, the walk back had seemed to last only a few minutes. Fortunately for Todd, no one on guard paid attention to him next to Jack.

Back in friendly territory, beneath the overhead netting and navigating the shallow trenches between tents, Jack bid Todd goodbye, and headed off to see Hailey. Before he'd even crossed the pit— occupied by Theo and Jen, busy loading up gear— Hailey found him.

The smile on her face puzzled him.

'What's up?' he asked, suspiciously.

'Come with me.' She turned to Theo. 'You too, Theo. Follow me.'

Theo shot Jack an inquisitive look and he shrugged in response. Jen looked annoyed, left with all the gear in the pit to sort through on her own, but didn't say anything as they followed Hailey.

Murphy and a stocky kid called Ade, who had a thick New York accent, were waiting when they arrived. Jack had barely spoken to Ade, but according to Theo, he had flown down to visit his grandparents just before the virus and was now essentially orphaned and in unfamiliar country.

Jack stood next to Ade and gave him a nod, which he returned. The big kid didn't look like he could run far, but he was nearly as tall as Jack with arms as thick as Jack's thighs, so he'd probably flatten most who got in his way. He'd have been a valuable addition to any defensive line.

Jack knew from observation that the kid rarely spoke.

'So,' Hailey announced. 'You're probably wondering why we're all here, given we've just had our loot run, huh?'

A few nods and murmurs.

'Well, the inventory count puts us a little short.'

'How short?' Theo asked.

'Well, a lot. We're also missing some extra gear, like medicine, which we couldn't find at the last location. Which means, we're going to need to do an emergency run.'

Jack leaned over the table, eyeing the map, but didn't spot anything marked out.

'Where are we going?' he asked.

Hailey took out a red pen and, under everyone's watchful gaze, drew a wide circle over a small place called Coldspring.

Chapter 7

Hailey knew the kids well enough to know they weren't stupid. They rarely missed a beat so, when she circled the town that had been forbidden territory for so long, five sets of eyes fell on her immediately.

Murphy was the first to speak up.

'Couldn't this get us killed? I thought the reason we were staying in the forest and only raiding the outskirts is that you wanted us on the down low?'

'I do, and this expedition won't get us killed, because we'll do it right.'

Robert was fixated on the map, frowning heavily.

'So, the reports of Chinese patrols there are wrong?'

'No,' Hailey said, rubbing the back of her neck. 'Those reports are accurate, but the patrols have been on the decrease for weeks now.'

Robert looked up.

'But they still do them? Why would we risk going there?'

'Because,' Jack interjected, 'it's time we stop hiding away.'

Hailey looked at Jack. She had seen the anger and torment brewing in him, and it seemed it was only a matter of time before he erupted. That was something to monitor, but for now she needed his confidence. It would bring the team together.

'He's right. This is our time to spread our wings. The forest won't sustain us forever, but that doesn't mean we can't do this smart. We've done this a hundred times since we've been here. We've worked well in small groups, had each other's backs, and stuck to the plan. And every time, we've come out okay.'

'Yeah, but we've never gone out that far,' Robert said. 'It's a larger town. Built-up. Lots of blind spots. What if we run into a patrol?'

Hailey nodded, beginning to pace up and down alongside the table.

'You're right. But we're armed, we're well trained and we aren't going in there with guns blazing. We're sneaking in and sneaking out, and with a bit of luck won't even see the hint of a Chinese soldier.'

Murphy walked around the table and pointed at the roads leading out from Coldspring.

'What's to say they aren't there in bigger numbers? Some of the roads are direct routes into places like Houston.'

'They're not,' Hailey replied.

'How do you know?'

'I've…' Hailey paused, then smiled at the group. 'I've scouted it already. Two nights ago.'

Theo shook his head.

'So that's where you were.'

Everyone started speaking at once, except Ade who stood like a rock, patiently, listening to everything.

Hailey eventually took control by clapping her hands.

'I've done this with intent, kids. I've done this with extremely thorough thought. If there was even a 10 per cent chance of us getting into trouble, I would tell Grandpa we'll just have to make do without the extra gear and supplies. But on this, I am certain. Coldspring is ours. It's the perfect time to swoop in, see what we can take, and leave. We'll do this by the cover of darkness, tonight, and—'

'Tonight!?' Robert whined.

Murphy cussed, then comically slapped a hand over her mouth. Even Jack was surprised at the urgency.

'Why us?' Ade said.

His deep voice quietened everyone. For someone who rarely uttered a word, Jack assumed when he did speak it was for something important.

'Because you're the oldest, fittest, best trained, smartest of the group. Best of the best. Scholarship dream team. Call it what you will. Grandpa and I have talked about this possibility and always had you six as the top pick.'

There was a pause as they counted.

'Five plus you?' Theo quizzed.

'No, I'm the seventh.'

'So… who's the sixth?' Murphy asked.

Hailey pointed behind them.

'Hey homies,' said Jessie, enthusiastically.

Throwing down three rucksacks in the dirt beside the table, she wiped her brow and tucked a wild blonde curl that had escaped her ponytail back behind her ears.

'Jessie's coming?' asked Robert. 'If I have this right, then all your best spotters are here? Isn't that leaving Camp Lisa a little vulnerable?'

'Nope,' said Jessie. 'Jen's just as good now, and there's still Bradley and Ruby who have been great doing the night watch. Don't let the fact they're freshmen throw your confidence.'

Hailey smiled at Jessie. *Good kid.*

***

Jack noticed the dissenting voices ended as abruptly as Jessie had arrived. Hailey organized the six she'd be taking to Coldspring into two groups, and had them triple check their packs, water and rations.

'No guns?' Theo asked, adjusting his backpack.

Jack had thought the same. Even if danger was relatively minimal, surely it'd be better to arm themselves in case of an incursion or a rogue patrol Hailey hadn't accounted for?

'No,' Hailey confirmed. 'The plan is stealth. Remember, nothing medium to long-range. If you see trouble—any of you—I want you to hold back, regroup and we'll evacuate immediately. If it's close range, then that's what your hunting knives are for.' She tapped the blade on her own hip. 'Cover the mouth and remember...'

'Throat or chest.' Everyone said in unison.

Hailey nodded.

'Throat or chest. What's our mantra for taking someone down?'

Some rolled their eyes, but Jack spoke up with everyone else. 'Cover the mouth, bury the blade, lower the body.'

'That's right. Cover, bury, lower. We don't want them screaming, or calling for help, and we sure don't want them making a noise falling. Don't forget, this is only in an ideal scenario. If you can't do any of this, just remember throat or chest.'

Robert shook his head.

'And what if all this training is for nothing, and we get overpowered?'

Theo leaned in, wrapping an arm around his neck as they headed toward Grandpa, who was waiting to see them off.

'Then, you give them everything you've got, Bobby boy.'

Grandpa met them at the edge of the camp, the ghost of a smile on his wrinkled features that didn't quite hide the concern there. He reached up, giving each of the kids a hug goodbye, before planting a kiss on Hailey's cheek and resting his forehead on hers.

'Bring them home safe, honey. And come back to me.'

Hailey cleared her throat.

'Will do, Pa.'

Coldspring was situated southeast of Camp Lisa and the park, so the first few hours of their long, hot hike in the late afternoon ran along the same trodden paths to the southern holiday camps they'd previously raided.

It wasn't until the sun dipped further and the air began to cool that they veered off the worn tracks and onto a new one.

Keeping quiet, he replayed the brief moment of Hailey and Grandpa's goodbye to each other, over in his head. He wished he didn't, but it was hard not to feel envy. He missed that feeling of being in the warm embrace of family, and with the envy came guilt at the times he'd pushed his mother away, embarrassed at the physical contact. What he wouldn't do now to go back and have every hug she'd ever offered.

Trapped again in one of his trademark reveries, he stumbled on a loose rock. Ade caught him and saved him from falling flat on his face.

'Thanks,' Jack said, brushing himself off and checking his ankle was fine.

'No problem.'

Thirty minutes later, their path led onto an old dirt track, which Hailey assured them would be fine to follow south for a while.

Hailey had explained before they left, that with such a long walk and the need to loot under the cover of darkness, they would make camp before sunset, sleep for a few hours, then rouse and enter

Coldspring.

Then, navigating each block in the shadows, they would spend two hours getting what they could, before disappearing back into the trees. They would hike an hour north, then make camp for the rest of the night. They couldn't risk tripping over each other or breaking legs in the dark.

Finally in the distance, they saw a parking lot.

'Okay, that lot leads onto the road to Coldspring,' said Hailey and motioned the group to backtrack a hundred yards, where they hunkered down in a thick stand of trees and started to pull out their gear.

Traveling extra light so they could maximize what they could carry back, each rolled out a single sleeping bag and tucked themselves in. To Jack's surprise, by the time his head hit the ground, he was out like a light. All too soon, though, he felt the jerk of someone shaking him awake.

'Wake up, Jack,' a voice whispered in his ear.

'Okay, okay,' he grumbled, extricating himself from the sleeping bag. It was a smiling Jessie who had roused him, already packed up and ready to go.

Yawning, he huddled up with the rest, falling in with Robert and Ade out in front, with Murphy and Theo bringing up the rear. Way out ahead, Jessie and Hailey led the pack.

When they reached the outskirts of Coldspring, Hailey signaled to Jack, Ade and Murphy to follow her. Jessie was to take Theo and Robert as a group of three. With the map and instructions for the stores to loot memorized, they said quiet goodbyes and parted ways.

Later when he looked back on the events that would follow, Jack wished he'd taken more time with the farewells that morning.

***

Lieutenant Wong shifted on his feet, smoothed his hair, and re-positioned his hat. Since the events outside Huntsville six months before, Colonel Jang li had kept him under close watch.

The first few weeks had been torturous. They'd lost the children they were hunting and an unacceptable number of soldiers into the bargain. And while that had been just as much Li's fault as his own, Wong had worn the brunt of the colonel's displeasure. It only got worse when Texas Command ordered Li's resources to Dallas to tend to an uprising.

Wong knew what stung most though was the fact Li had been forced to turn tail and flee for his life, chased by an old propeller-driven plane.

Now, deep into the awful, dry, Texan summer, Li, still under pressure from General Wang Hao to find the killers of his daughter, was as desperate as ever to find the America brats and whether he liked it or not, Wong was along for the ride.

When he had worked up the courage, he took a deep breath and knocked twice. The command to enter came immediately and he stepped in, already feeling nervous sweat prickling his brow.

Jang Li looked up from the array of computer monitors on his desk and locked his gaze on Wong's.

'What is it?'

'Colonel, I—'

Jang Li raised a hand slowly, and Wong shut his mouth quickly. He was obedient now. Like a whipped mutt. Gone were the days he felt brave enough to kill a lowly corporal.

'Coldspring?'

Wong's eyes widened.

'Yes Colonel, I have reports—'

'Lieutenant Wong. Remember who you are speaking to.'

Wong bowed his head.

'Yes, Colonel. Sorry.'

'I have a two-man patrol traveling from Huntsville to Coldspring as we speak. They are under orders not to engage. I'll soon know if it's the children we are looking for and we can take more… drastic action.'

'But how did you know?' Wong blurted.

'You think I don't have access to the same information as you? Don't be stupid Wong,' Li said turning back to his screens.

Wong didn't know whether to thank him or even if he was dismissed, but his lingering irritated Jang Li, who waved his hand impatiently.

Wong rushed from the room, closing the door behind him, and let out a sigh. He didn't know how Li had found out about the satellite images at Coldspring when he'd only just taken the report himself, but hopefully it was those they sought and there would be a swift end to the matter. Wong longed for Li to return to the west coast where he belonged.

Chapter 8

Valero gas station. Valero gas station, Jack repeated silently.

The plan was to reconvene by the painted shed next to the Valero gas station in three hours and leave via the woods.

Jessie and her team had gone right, down Alpine Street toward what Hailey said was the county jail, while they went straight ahead. The plan would be to take a block each side, to avoid missing anything and maximize opportunity within the short timeframe.

Hailey led Jack, Ade, and Murphy down Byrd Avenue—the main artery through Coldspring—making sure to keep close to the shadows of buildings where it was darkest.

The Chinese army had seen fit to shut down the electricity grids of any towns or areas that were of no immediate value to them. Even though it had been months since he'd been within sight of a town or city, Jack found the pervading darkness amidst the trappings of civilization weird and off-putting.

It was clear that Coldspring was, at best, a name on a map and nothing more to the invaders, which should mean they would remain unbothered on this expedition.

Keeping his breathing steady and watching where he walked, Jack's eyes soon adjusted to the pitch-black night, and he made out widely-spaced business units and old storefronts as they approached the center of town.

To add to the sense of strangeness he felt, close to the town center they passed an old whitewashed church built from bricks and timber, the kind you'd expect to see on a dusty lot out in the Wild West.

The further they walked, the more built up the sides of the avenue became. On the right, a few cafés, bars, and grills, and on the left, offices, a discount store and another café.

Jack's stomach growled at the images in the windows of the restaurants.

'I'll have a flame-grilled steak with fries and slaw on the side, with a cold glass of coke,' Jack said quietly.

'Amen to that. But with onion rings, you know?' said Murphy.

Hailey shushed them and pointed to a building two doors down, the first they would work tonight.

'You two take that one.'

Above the windows, the signage in black lettering read 'Peter Mason – Attorney At Law'. Jack frowned—why were they going into an attorney's office?

'Just go look,' said Hailey. 'You never know.'

Hailey led Ade next door into a café.

Jack tested the lawyer's office door gingerly. The cold brass handle turned easily and he pushed the door open.

He looked back at Murphy, who motioned impatiently for him to enter. He stepped over the threshold and let Murphy in before closing the door. Inside the darkened room on polished timber floorboards stood a single desk cluttered with papers, a computer monitor and a phone.

Behind it, Jack and Murphy saw there were two rows of cubicles with dual-monitors, and filing cabinets crowding the small alcoves.

They rummaged through the desk draws and cabinets and quickly turned up nothing. It was difficult in the darkness but Hailey had warned them only to use the flashlights sparingly, and even then only in enclosed rooms, so light wouldn't be seen directly from the street.

'This is bullshit,' muttered Jack, pulling out his flashlight to cast the light around the storeroom they'd found at the back.

'What are you doing?' whispered Murphy. 'Hailey said...'

'I know what she said, but we can't see a damn thing. Look. There's nothing here but papers and... hang on.'

Jack's flashlight found a cabinet door above a kitchenette at the rear, ajar. When he opened it, he found a stash of pills in two small jars. Peering at the labels, he saw one was Xanax and the other Diazepam.

Score.

'Look here,' Jack smiled. 'Meds. Not a total bust.'

Murphy nodded and gave him a thumbs up as he stuffed them into his backpack. Besides the meds, they found nothing else except instant coffee, sugar and an open packet of stale Oreos.

'We done here?' asked Jack.

'Sure. Let's go.'

Leaving the lawyer's, they saw Hailey and Ade move on to the bar and grill. Murphy and Jack chose to cross the street to search the Italian restaurant.

Inside, the décor was garish and over the top. Jack moved his flashlight around, taking in the maroon wallpaper and gold filigree.

'Hope their food was good because the décor left a lot to be desired.'

Murphy sniggered.

In the kitchen they found a large stash of condiments and salt, which they took, and also a gallon bottle each of cooking oil. Near the back of the kitchen where the big refrigerator door was ajar, a horrific stench had them both gagging.

'Shit,' Jack swore, putting a hand to his mouth. 'What is that?'

'Fish and meat rotting away is my guess. No power, it all goes off. Must have been sitting there going bad for months.'

Jack dry-retched and pushed past Murphy.

'Sure you don't wanna check it out?' Murphy laughed. 'Could be—'

'*No*. Nuh-uh. Let's just go. We're good.'

On the way out, Murphy ducked into the manager's office and found a medical kit sitting on the desk, which she promptly slipped into her loot sack.

They exited the restaurant and continued along their side of the street, keeping pace with Hailey and Ade's progress on the other side.

Distracted by the task at hand and with no sign of any Chinese patrols or even any evidence they had been in the town, Jack's nervousness had subsided by the time they reached the discount grocer's store. In fact, he was feeling downright confident.

This was what he had needed. Bigger risk, for a bigger reward.

Jack and Murphy's feet creaked on a section of old sidewalk patched together with new timber palings. They trod carefully, eased open the shop door to keep it from ringing the bell, and stepped inside.

Like in the kitchen of the restaurant, odor assaulted their senses, but nothing as revolting as the spoiled meat and fish. This smell was mustier, and he figured there wouldn't have been much fresh food beside fruit and vegetables or things like bread.

Across all the shelves and stacks at the back, a fine coat of dust covered everything. Here, between the shadowed isles of groceries and hardware goods, Jack lost himself.

This was their biggest score yet.

Into the backpack, he threw tools, string, tape, paper, batteries, scissors, knives. Then in the next aisle, he found some canned goods. Flicking on his flashlight, through dust particles dancing in the hazy beam of light, he scored a half dozen cans of mac n cheese.

'Hey, Murph!' he called out.

No answer.

'Murph?'

Nothing.

Jack felt a surge of adrenaline and his breathing quickened. With his heart racing, he crouched down in the aisle, turned his flashlight off and reached for his knife. Edging towards the end of the aisle, he peeked around the corner towards the checkouts.

Nothing.

Where the hell was she?

He turned to find a shadowy figure standing over him. Jack fell onto his ass as the figure burst out laughing. It was Murphy. She stood over him, with her flashlight under her chin highlighting her facial features in a ghoulish fashion.

Jack gave silent thanks that he hadn't screamed.

'Murphy! Not funny,' he said. 'I could have killed you.'

'Yeah sure. What, like this?' she laughed, mimicking Jack falling over.

'Bite me,' he said, laughing.

'No thanks.'

The playful bickering went on as they collected a few more items before heading out and meeting up with Hailey and Ade back at the next street corner.

'What's that, the town hall?' Jack asked, pointing to the large, three-story brick building with a wide stone staircase leading up to the entrance.

'County courthouse, I think,' said Hailey

'Are we going in there?' Murphy asked, adjusting the straps on her already sagging backpack.

'No,' she said, looking down the street that bisected the one they were on. Church Street. 'We'll go that way and hopefully link up with the others if they're done on their side of town.

'Sounds good,' Ade said.

Jack had meant to quiz Hailey, figuring a huge building like the courthouse might have something they could use. But when Ade gave it his rare verbal seal of approval, he let it go.

Hailey led them on, passing a Taco place on the right that tortured Jack's appetite with a memory of the Tuesday taco nights he shared with his family nearly every week of his childhood.

***

Private Xiang spat into the tall grass, adjusting the rifle on his shoulder, and looked over at Sheng. Sheng was taller, better looking and always got the favor of their Lieutenant. But Xiang had always outmatched him in one area.

Hand-to-hand combat.

Smiling to himself, as they approached yet another back-water American town on orders from above, Xiang cocked his head to Sheng and laughed.

'This assignment sucks ass. Want to make things more interesting.'

Sheng groaned and gave his reply through gritted teeth.

'I'm not fighting you again, Xiang.'

'Why not?'

Sheng shook his head and picked up his pace. Xiang matched it.

'Come on,' Xiang persisted, passing an old parking lot, filled with abandoned cars outside a donut shop. The yanks sure loved their dance with diabetes.

'You see,' Sheng said, stopping on the sidewalk and shouldering his rifle, well aware of Xiang's jealousy. 'This is why Lieutenant Wong favors me over you. You are undisciplined.'

'No, that's not why.'

'Yes, it is. You're a loose cannon.'

'No,' Xiang insisted, leaning in and pointing a finger, taking a hand away from his rifle. 'It's because Wong knows your family and wants to give you an easy ride up the ranks.'

Sheng's eyes narrowed in anger.

'I think that's enough.'

He turned without a second word and continued up the street, passing a school on their left.

Xiang smirked, knowing he'd hit a nerve. Lifting

his rifle back up into position, he fell back into step with Sheng, and focused on the long road ahead. While he never said a word against orders from command out loud, he had asked why they had to park their vehicle so far outside Coldspring.

'To avoid detection, no doubt,' Sheng had offered, as they climbed out of their seats a few miles back.

It was the only thing that made sense. They were ordered in for a reason, but only two of them so it couldn't be anything too exciting. Maybe a handful of escapee children.

Regardless, the patrol and the walking it entailed would do him good. Ever since they had reassigned him to the fueling facility they had set up north of Houston, all he had done was stand and guard.

The level of boredom since they had squashed nearly all of the pockets of rebellious children and teenagers was unprecedented. What he wouldn't do for some excitement even if it was just to go into the city.

He wished they'd built the damn thing *in* Houston by the docks or something, but according to those high above, the open landscape to the north gave them the perfect opportunity to efficiently guard and oversee the facility. It was also close enough to the cluster of oil refineries they had rebooted in Houston and the road network to Dallas and beyond to help provide for the people's army in the southern quadrant.

Still, they were out on patrol now, and hopefully there would be plenty of these little excursions to break the monotony of simple guard duty.

Xiang blinked. Ahead, in the dark, amongst the sparse buildings of Coldspring, he noticed a flicker of light.

'Sheng.'

'I saw it too,' he said, looking at him.

Xiang nodded. 'Let's go check it out.'

Chapter 9

Robert yanked on the vault door with one hand but it was too heavy. He put the handle of his compact flashlight between his teeth, and grabbed it with both hands, pulling with all his strength.

'You know that's never gonna open, right?' Theo chuckled from behind him, lurking in the dark with his own flashlight off.

Theo had super vision or something. Not Robert. He needed the flashlight as much as possible. He gave the vault door one last tug before he gave up, picking up his backpack.

'I still think you should turn your flashlight off, dude. The whole point is stealth.'

Jessie's dark shape materialized from behind Theo.

'He's right,' she said. 'We can't afford it. And you've been using the damn thing since we started.'

Robert rubbed his eyes.

'Fine.'

When he switched it off, he had to blink several times to adjust to the dark, but still had to put his hands out to feel where he was going. His night vision really did suck. Before the virus had hit America, his mother had made an appointment with an eye doctor for him, then of course, the world had ended.

'Good job,' Theo said. 'Let's get out of here. There's a place across from here we can check out.'

'Okay,' said Robert. 'I'll meet you guys out front. I need to hit the head.'

'Ew,' Jessie said. 'See you out front.'

Theo followed Jessie out to the main foyer, and Robert turned back, passing the vault and heading into a corridor that led to a fire exit. Pushing it open he tensed, almost expecting an alarm to go off. He went out into what had been a staff parking lot, now overgrown with weeds, and unzipped, taking a leak against the building. It was a long one—he had been busting for at least 20 minutes— and to pass time, he tried to get his aim as high up the wall as possible.

Satisfied with his efforts, he zipped himself up and looked around. Across the lot was a line of trees. A light July breeze ruffled the oak leaves, and the tall grass around them.

He inhaled a deep draft of fresh air, his mood considerably improved compared to the start of the mission, then headed back into the bank, not bothering to pull the door closed behind him. After all, who was left to care about a bank with open doors?

***

Sheng raised a hand as they approached the bank, rifles at the ready. The light had gone out, but they knew someone was inside.

With a motion of his hand, Sheng told Xiang to go to the left side of the building to flank, while he would skirt low across the parking lot to the right.

Using a hedge and the darkness for cover, the two soldiers moved into position. Xiang steadied his breathing and peered into the window to check for signs of life.

Sure enough, standing in the main lobby, clueless at the danger they were in, were two Americans. A tall white teenage boy and a shorter girl next to him. Xiang often forgot what their engineered attack had done to the populace. Still one of the youngest recruits, Xiang was 20 and easily a handful of years senior to these kids.

Still, they would need to be dealt with.

Xiang looked across the edge of the building and caught Sheng's attention. He raised a hand gesturing into the lobby and raised two fingers. Sheng nodded, extended his hand, fingers out, and then curled a finger and brought his arm back up.

Time.

***

Back inside the dark building, Robert navigated the short corridor, passing the door to the storeroom, the vault, and two offices. When he turned the corner, with a line of sight to the front of the building and the moonlit foyer, his stomach dropped to the floor.

There, beyond Theo and Jessie, a silhouetted figure with a rifle charged through the bank doors, screaming in Mandarin. A yell of warning stuck in his throat, and he ducked back behind the corner, his heart trying to hammer its way out of his ribcage. He heard a violent scuffle, followed by a single burst of gunfire then a cry of anguish.

Robert couldn't move. He was frozen. Paralyzed with fear and indecision. Soldiers, but how many? Footsteps approached his position. Jen's face floated into his mind's eye and he pulled out his hunting knife, gripping it hard like it was his last link to reality.

This was it, he thought. They had killed Theo and Jessie, and now they were coming for him.

He swallowed, closed his eyes and stood up to his full height. He could do this. He wasn't a coward. *Throat or chest. Throat or chest.*

The footsteps approached the corner of the corridor. Robert raised his blade, surged around the corner, and ran at the soldier standing just feet away.

***

Jessie spat blood out onto the foyer carpet and crawled her way over to Theo, who lay beside the fallen soldier. He wasn't shot, just knocked out. Luckily, the soldier hadn't just opened fire—Theo had taken a rifle butt to the head, but thanks to his misguided attempt to subdue them, she had been able to slash the soldier's throat before he had turned and fired, his bullets spraying harmlessly into the ceiling as he dropped to his knees and tried to stem the torrent of blood squirting from his carotid.

Dazed but on high alert, she looked around and spied another soldier creeping towards the back of the building, gun raised.

Robert!

She scrambled for the Chinese soldier's gun but slipped in his blood. It was too far away, and it was too late.

Jessie watched helpless as Robert burst into sight and ran at the soldier who simply raised his gun and fired a short burst into Robert's chest. The boy flew backwards, landing in a crumpled heap. Jessie choked on her cry, whimpering into her hand to stifle the sound. She crawled fast, toward the discarded rifle.

A shout of Mandarin alerted her. The murdering soldier had seen her and was sprinting towards her, his rifle pointed and ready to fire. Still a few feet from the gun, Jessie accepted her fate, put her hands up and closed her eyes, waiting for the end.

***

When Jack and the others heard the commotion, they were already close. Very close.

'Go!' yelled Hailey, breaking into a sprint.

They charged after her towards the source of the screams and gunfire. Outside the bank, they tore across the road to the right side of the building and flattened themselves against the still warm bricks.

Hailey turned to Jack and pulled out a Glock

from her waistband. How had he not seen that?

'No time to explain. Jack, Murphy, take the fire exit at the back. Ade, come with me. I will draw them to the front, and you two take the rear. Remember what we learned about stealth, okay?'

'Got it.'

A single burst of gunfire rang out from inside the bank, and their faces blanched white in the dark.

'Go!' Hailey mouthed and turned away from them, charging around to the front with Abe.

Jack took off the opposite way with Murphy, skidding on some gravel in the back lot, clutching at the wall for support. With his heart in his mouth and his senses on alert, he lunged for the partially open fire exit door and charged in.

Inside, Jack and Murphy crouched low as they ran up the corridor. They paused before the corner, peeking around it. Jack's eyes were drawn immediately to the shape on the floor.

'Oh… God no… Robert…'

'No…' Murphy moaned into the back of her hand as she saw.

Robert's chest was a ragged, bloody mess, his eyes wide open and staring lifelessly at the ceiling.

Jack felt bile in his throat but swallowed it down and looked towards the foyer.

Ahead of them, a single soldier stood over three figures. Two of the shapes lay on the floor unmoving and the other was on their haunches with arms raised in surrender.

Jessie...

Murphy's unexpected sob attracted the attention of the soldier and he spun around to point the rifle their way. Jack forced Murphy behind him, shielding her from the imminent hail of bullets when, not a second too late, Hailey ran through the front door, her Glock raised, and emptied it into the soldier's back as he squeezed the trigger.

Hot metal stitched the wall next to Jack, spitting fragments of concrete and dust into his face before he and Murphy dove to the floor.

When it was safe, he looked up. The soldier was down, and Hailey was racing over to Jessie. He climbed to his feet and helped Murphy up before crossing over to them.

He realized the crumpled bodies were Theo and another Chinese soldier.

Shit, he thought. *Not Theo, too.*

A groan disabused him of that idea as Theo stirred awake, putting a hand to his head.

'Arrgh!' he moaned. 'My head...'

'Ade,' Hailey ordered. 'Help Theo. We need to go. Now.' Hailey held out a hand and helped Jessie up. When Jack had made it over, he noticed Jessie's hand was clasping her side, her shirt soaked in blood.

'Shit... Jessie. You're hurt...'

'It's not mine,' she began looking down, the realized that there was a bloody rip in her t-shirt. 'Oh, I think he got me...'

Jack took off his backpack and rummaged for the medical kit they had looted just an hour previous. He pulled it out and started removing bandages and gauze from the packaging.

'Hurry, we don't know if there are more,' Hailey urged as she lifted Jessie's shirt and inspected the bloody furrow. 'Bullet didn't go in, just nicked her. Patch it quickly.'

She stood up, checked her magazine and slotted it back in, before chambering another round. 'I'll keep an eye outside in case we have any more visitors. Get her patched and we go.'

A strangled voice behind them stopped Hailey.

'W-what about… what about Robert?' Murphy said.

Hailey's face fell and she shook her head. No words needed. They would have to leave him. Murphy burst into tears, and Hailey left them, with Ade offering to take one of the enemy rifles and guard the back entrance, which Hailey agreed to.

Inside, with just the sound of Murphy's muted sobs, Theo nursed his head whilst Jack tried his best to patch Jessie up.

'Ah!' she cried out, as he used some alcohol to dab at the wound.

'Sorry,' he said. 'Got to clean it before we go.'

Not making a pretty job of it, Jack hastily wrapped bandages around her abdomen area, and taped it down tight. Checking the bleeding was under control, he stuffed the gear back into his backpack, helped Jessie up, and walked out front with Theo and Murphy in tow.

'Right,' Jack said, letting out a breath he didn't realize he was holding. 'We're good to go.'

Hailey let out a whistle, and a few seconds later, Ade came jogging around from the side of the bank.

'Right then?' she said grimly, examining them all, biting her bottom lip. Jack had the impression she was trying with all her might to hold it together. 'Let's go.'

Their exit from Coldspring was slow and methodical. Not only did they have the wounded Jessie to support, but they were also careful to stick to shadows and check their surrounds every 50 yards. They reached their campsite in 30 minutes but Hailey kept them moving.

It was so far so good, but there was no telling if there were any more soldiers around or soon to arrive and they couldn't risk stopping.

Robert's lifeless eyes haunted Jack, bringing back fresh feelings of grief and failure as he walked the dark track, plowing on ahead of the others. Hailey had to ask him several times to slow down.

After a half-hour, Jack flicked his flashlight to better see the overgrown path. No one protested; they were now far enough out from the town with no sign nor sound of pursuit.

Jack turned to Hailey just once on their seemingly endless march back to Camp Lisa. In the pale moonlight that filtered down through the forest canopy, he could see her cheeks were stained with tears.

PART 2: OPERATION UNDERDOG

Chapter 10

As they arrived home, the red sun was rising like a bloody wound over the horizon. Exhausted both physically and mentally, Jack crumpled when they arrived in the main trenches, dropping his gear, and staring ahead.

Grandpa met Hailey ahead of him and after some low conversation they led Jessie and Theo to the medical tent for treatment.

A hand touched his shoulder then, and he flinched before looking up to see it was Ade. The single tear that ran down his cheek said more than any words could. Jack stood up and gave his big campmate a hug but before he could finish and break away, he felt Ade tense.

'Where's Robert?' asked a soft voice behind them.

Jack felt his stomach sink like a stone and turned to find a pale-faced Jen looking at him.

Jack's mouth opened but no words could find a way past the lump in his throat. In the end, he could only offer a shake of his head.

'*Noooo!*'

Jen's howl of anguish was unearthly and before Jack could go to her, she turned on her heels and ran back towards the females' living quarters. Jack bowed his head as once again Ade's hand fell on his shoulder.

Suddenly angry at the unfairness of it all, he shook Ade's hand off and stomped off towards his own tent. His movements, like those of Jen, were tracked by dozens of concerned eyes and he was glad to duck into the tent he had shared with Robert.

He collapsed onto his sleeping bag and rolled over, his eyes falling on Robert's sleeping area, everything neat and tidy just the way he liked it.

He wept then. Not just for Robert, but for Jen and his sister, Katie. For his Mom and Dad. For Danny, and everyone since. He curled up in a ball, knees up to his chin, and wept quietly.

He wasn't sure how long he lay there, but a rustling at the tent opening snapped him out of his reverie. Jack turned over and found Grandpa's worn face looking in at him.

'How are you doing, kid?'

Jack sniffed, sitting up.

'Better. Just... I... I felt like... I dunno.'

Grandpa crawled in and sat next to him, putting an arm around his shoulders.

'It's okay not to have words for it. I came here to say sorry.'

'Sorry?' Jack looked up. Confused. 'What for?'

'For being the one to orchestrate this and having to put your lives in danger. I should have been there with you.'

'It's fine, Grandpa.'

'No it ain't, kid. None of this is right. None of

it.' The old man sighed, a sound from deep in his chest. He seemed to have aged 10 years overnight, withered and tired from the news. 'I wish things were different, Jack, I really do. The virus. The invasion. And now the things we have to do just to survive. A year ago, no one would have believed Hollywood science fiction would become our day-to-day.' Another deep breath, this one hitching in his throat. 'I've seen too many kids die...'

Jack saw his eyes welling up.

'This is not on you, Grandpa. You saved us. Without this sanctuary you started we'd all be dead—or worse, slaves.'

The pair sat in silence for a while longer before Grandpa finally got to his feet.

'I talked to Jen. It will take her a while to grieve, so be patient with her, this has hit her harder than any of us.'

Jack nodded.

As with any ailment, sometimes the best remedy was to keep busy. And so, he did. When he emerged from his tent, Jack immersed himself in camp chores. He loaded and organized gear and supplies, cleaned weapons, and even chopped firewood.

By the late afternoon, the sleepless night and emotional strain caught up on him again, and after eating a light and extremely late lunch, he went back to his tent and slept.

It was a restless slumber, filled with the faces of

the dead, and screams in the dark. When he jerked to, covered in a sheen of sweat, he found he was not alone. Murphy was sitting beside him.

'Murph?' he groaned, rubbing his eyes.

It was dark outside. He'd slept through dinner and into the night. For how long, he couldn't say, but he didn't feel hungry, or rested.

'Come,' she said. 'You need to see this.'

Jack followed Murphy out of the tent and then around the edges of the cluster of tents, and onto the well-worn path between the trees on the western side of camp that led to the pond, a small body of water in a clearing just a quarter mile from Camp Lisa.

'Where are we going,' Jack asked, wondering if Murphy was confused. She didn't answer, but in the distance, between the trunks of the Sam Houston forest, he saw the glow of lights. He didn't press her.

When they emerged from the shadows of the trees, there, by the small pond, stood all the survivors. Every single one of them.

On the water, were a fleet of tiny paper boats containing small candles—a farewell to Robert. Jack heard soft weeping and prayers as he weaved his way to the water and found himself next to Jen.

The bobbing of candlelight on the water repelled the encroaching darkness. Jack took Jen's hand and they stood silently with the survivors, listening until one by one, people completed their prayers and words, and returned to Camp Lisa.

Soon, only Jack and Jen remained.

'Jen,' he said, daring to speak after what seemed like forever. 'I'm... I'm so sorry.'

She squeezed his hand then turned to him, her eyes filled with tears. The hug she gave him was brief and she broke away almost immediately before heading back to camp.

He didn't follow her. The small gestures were enough to tell him that she didn't blame him for what had happened and being alone by the pond with the flotilla of candles was oddly comforting.

He sat on the shore and watched the bobbing memorial to Robert for two hours before finally heading back to his sleeping roll.

Operation Underdog was delayed by a week to allow everyone to come to grips with the deadly setback at Coldspring. In the meantime, Hailey hardened the message and expectations about the raid on the fuel depot.

'You know what happened at Coldspring,' she said two nights out. 'I need you to understand it can happen again and maybe much worse. Hell, its possible none of us will come back. If any of you want out, tell me now.'

No one wanted out.

A week later, at the breaking of dawn, just hours before Operation Underdog would officially commence, Jack rose from his bedroll with an ache in his neck, and a stomach full of butterflies.

He told Hailey how he felt, as he was helping her

load stuff into the truck they would, for the first time in months, drive out from their hideout to the outskirts of Houston.

In her typical, blunt, Texan way, she reminded Jack to control his emotions.

'I know you're excited,' she said, heaving a box of ammunition onto the flatbed. 'But you need to control those nerves and focus on the job at hand. We need cool, quick-thinking heads.'

'I will,' Jack said.

'Good.'

Jack felt her eyes on him as he walked back to load more gear into the truck. The plan had only been revealed to members of the team. In the awful scenario that Camp Lisa was overrun in their absence, people taken as hostage and tortured for information wouldn't be able to disclose their location or plans.

Driving south, they would take the smaller roads to the outskirts of Houston. There, they would go off-road with the truck, and stash it in trees or a derelict building and continue on foot. They would split weapons and gear between them and leave some heavier weapons in the truck. In the event things went south, and survivors made it back to the truck, they'd probably have pursuers hot on their heels and would need the firepower.

When they were packed and ready, Grandpa said a few words.

'Well, this is it kids. If this goes to shit and you're separated from the rest of the team, I want you to hunker down until you have a way clear. If you can, head back to the truck or worst case, get the hell out and try and make your way back to camp on foot. Once you're in, don't take any chances. Truth is, folks, you gotta roll in quiet as cats, do the job and then get out of there lickety-split.'

Finally, just before noon, the last of their gear was loaded and everyone had time to clean, check and load their weapons. Each member of the team had been given a handgun and assault rifle, with the intent they would be used as an absolute last resort.

They were to go in quiet and get out loud.

Throwing his backpack up into the truck, Jack was the last one in, helped up by Theo and Ade, who made light work of his 190-pound build. Sitting on crates, they looked back at Grandpa and the camp.

'Are you sure you don't want to come along for the fun, Grandpa?' a smiling Theo asked, eliciting a roll of the eyes from Murphy, who sat next to him.

Grandpa smirked, pulling out a walkie-talkie.

'No can do, Son, someone has to keep an eye on things here,' he said. Then into the walkie-talkie, 'you're good to go, honey.'

'Roger,' came the reply through a burst of static.

'What'll you do if we don't…?' Murphy started.

'You'll come back,' said the old man, finishing the incomplete question. 'Six months of training weren't for nothing, you hear? Besides, I still got old Betsy, should the worst happen.'

'Oh yeah, I forgot about your old bird.'

Grandpa saluted, which drew smiles from all around the truck. From inside the driver's cabin, Hailey raised an arm from the window and tapped the roof.

'Alright then, you be safe,' Grandpa waved. 'And see you soon.'

A group of other survivors, including Jen, waved them off, some of their faces etched with worry, and Jack was glad when they turned out of sight.

As the truck rumbled along, he glanced down at the handgun, ejecting the magazine and checking it was fully loaded before sliding it home again.

While he didn't plan to disobey orders and open fire unless necessary, he decided he would take as many of the assholes out as he could before he bit the dust if things went ass up.

The truck jerked as Hailey steered it south from the camp, and trundled on toward Houston, where the next chapter in their fight for survival would begin.

Chapter 11

Colonel Jang Li's cigarette smoke dissipated in the warm night air. He stood off a side road of hard-packed dirt and weeds. With little in the way of trees or buildings, a gust of wind rumbled over the fields and stirred the hair on Li's head.

Squinting out into the dark and taking another drag, he spotted a man slinking out from the tall grass, breaking into a slow jog when he reached the road.

'Private Xu,' Jang Li spoke, flicking ash to his side and noticing he was alone. He had expected all three of them. 'Where are Xiang and Sheng?'

The soldier stiffened, trying to catch his breath. He was a short, slim man with a buzz cut close to the scalp. His small frame was exactly why he had been picked for this particular role. Quick and easy to disappear.

'They missed the rendezvous, Sir,' Xu said.

'Did you wait long?'

A nod. 'Yes Sir. Two hours, Sir.'

'Did your source have anything to say on the matter?'

'Yes,' the private said, looking scared to continue.

'Tell me.'

'My informant confirmed that two People's Army soldiers were killed in Coldspring and that they also lost one of their own.'

'Hmm.'

This wasn't ideal. Not ideal at all, if word from their guerilla camp was to be believed. Jang Li needed to present better findings to General Wang Hao, so he pressed on.

'And did you obtain the details about the planned attack, I-'

'Yes Sir but-' Xu interrupted.

Jang Li lashed out and slapped his subordinate across the face. As quick as his anger had appeared, it subsided, and he threw his cigarette away.

'Do not interrupt me again.'

'Yes Sir...'

'But what?' he sighed, turning and walking back toward the main road, the private marching in his wake.

'One of the three you seek is dead. He was killed in the engagement with Xiang and Sheng.'

'I see. Pity, I wanted to torture all three of them. Was it the girl?'

'No Sir. The taller of the two boys. Not the leader.'

Li nodded.

Good.

'So, the target is the fuel facility?'

'Yes Sir,' said Xu, not sure if he should proceed.

'Speak idiot! When, where?!'

'My source confirmed it will be tomorrow night. He wasn't privy to the conversations, but he said it was easy to spy on them. He confirmed the terrorists plan to blow up the facility with a team of six. The boy, the leader of the three escapees, will be amongst them. His name is Jack.'

Li nodded thoughtfully.

'Excellent work Xu. The General will be pleased with this. If your source is correct and we thwart the teenage idiots and capture this boy, you may just earn yourself a medal for your good work.'

Xu's eyes widened.

'Yes Sir,' he said, puffing his chest out and saluting.

'For your sake though,' Jang Li said, leaning over him. 'Let's hope your little traitor in that camp isn't feeding you disinformation. I would hate for your family to lose... such a valuable source of income. That would be tragic.'

Turning away from the private he walked to the black limousine and climbed in.

'Drive,' he said and gestured to his bodyguard. The man carefully poured him a tumbler of his favored American Whisky and handed it to him.

Li smiled as he swirled the valuable contraband in his mouth. Tomorrow evening he would finally deliver on his promise to capture the murderer of his daughter.

With his head tilted back, nose to the wind, Jack basked in the warmth of the sun and took in deep breaths of air. He wanted to savor the day just a little more, because he knew full well it could possibly be his last.

The roar of the truck had become a comforting rumble that was only interrupted by groans of the gears when they slowed and veered off the road to negotiate their way around abandoned cars.

Along the way south, they saw the occasional body. Some more recent than others, but most thoroughly decomposed by the Texan sun.

Jack turned back from the road after the last one, a small boy whose eyes had been picked out by birds, his throat suddenly feeling awfully dry. He hunkered down and rummaged for the water flask.

'Don't go finishing that off all at once,' said Murphy.

Jack made an exaggerated show of sipping just a little, smacking his lips, before twisting the cap back on the flask.

'Happy?'

Murphy raised an eyebrow.

'Sorry,' he said. 'I'm feeling a little tense.'

'No shit,' Theo said, his chin in his hand, as he gazed over the fields that whipped by.

Since they'd left, a few of their company had grown agitated, whilst others, like Jack, had fallen into a serene, fatalistic kind of state.

From inside the cabin of the truck, Hailey reached a hand out, slamming the top of the roof, which signaled to the survivors in the flatbed to hold tight.

On cue, she took a sharp left off the asphalt, down a short decline, and onto a long, bumpy dirt track heading toward a spattering of oak trees and grass. Beside it, about five minutes down the track, a few old farm buildings loomed and Jack realized the spot would be a perfect base to hide their gear for the return journey.

He clung to that particular dream with both hands.

The return journey.

When the truck stopped and they climbed out, Jack stood back to drink it in. The blue Ford, nestled beneath the low branch of an oak tree, hidden behind the north-facing wall of an old farmhouse, the rust-red paint flaking off its wooden cladding.

They'd make it. They had to.

Theo pushed a heavy crate of ammo into his chest.

'Don't just stand around, bro.'

'Sorry,' he said and carried the heavy box into the barn, dumping it with the rest of the equipment.

The entire group worked silently, happy to let the chore occupy their thoughts from the dangerous task in front of them. Jack noticed Hailey making sure everything was stacked neatly, even taking time to redo some of the stacks.

Ade seemed most at ease. The man of few words seemed so at peace with everything that was happening that it almost began to annoy Jack.

What is this guy's deal?

'All of you,' Hailey shouted before Jack had a chance to ask Ade his secret. 'Into the barn. Now.'

Hailey disappeared back inside, and the rest of them followed her.

Laid out on the boxes that she was using as a make-shift table, Hailey had placed a big map, weighed down by two boxes of ammunition. There were various lines and circles drawn on the paper.

They gathered around, most perspiring from the heat in the poorly ventilated barn.

'This is where we are now,' Hailey said, her voice echoing amongst the rafters above. She pointed to a spot just a few miles from the outskirts of Houston, amongst farms, sparse suburbs and woodland. 'And this is the shiny new fuel facility the Chinese built.'

She jabbed the pen about three or more miles southeast of their position at a blank spot on the map.

'It looks like vacant land on the map, but I can assure you, there's a full operation going on there. The facilities already in place were destroyed by Americans before the virus took full effect, so they had to start from scratch. Along with imports from their other bases of operation, this one facility provides all the gas needs for the People's Army in the state of Texas.

'So,' Hailey continued. 'You've heard it all before. We've run the plan, but this is crunch time, so I'm going to run it again so we are all clear on mission objective, okay?'

Nods all around the table. Jack's heart was starting to pump faster now. This was it. No going back.

'Good.'

Hailey jumped straight into the strategy of the mission, explaining the crucial need for formation, stealth, and non-verbal communication. She reiterated on the map the entry points to the facility, and the exit point to meet—if all went well.

Then, she explained about the charges. With little or no experience with explosives, the group would have to rely on instruction and mindfulness when placing the C4 they had accumulated. They wouldn't need to use a lot if things went well— they were igniting fuel after all—but with such a small amount, the chain-reaction would be crucial.

Repeating herself three times, Hailey showed them one by one how to place the charges and set the timers.

With the plan run through and workshop on C4 complete, they picked up their weapons. Even though they had been cleaned the morning before, Hailey insisted on checking them again, with Jessie watching everyone to make sure they were doing as they were told. There would be no safe margin of error.

Jack, now worryingly comfortable with firearms, did his in record time, and stood ready, with his silencers attached.

Jessie then went person to person and applied black paint to their exposed skin.

'Remember,' Hailey said, when Jessie finished applying the face paint. 'The silencers will not muffle the shots like the movies. They'll still make a hell of a pop. So, last resort, okay? I want you to all show me your knives, just to be sure.'

On command, they unsheathed their hunting knives, holding them up for Hailey to see.

Jack watched as Hailey armed herself, tying her hair back into a black hat, which had been offered to Murphy, Jessie and Theo, whose own hair had grown out a little.

They exited the barn, shut the doors and walked to the edge of the yard. The sun was now setting on the horizon and a chorus of crickets filled the late afternoon.

'It's a three-mile hike,' said Hailey. 'Just under an hour if we keep a steady pace. I don't want bunching, so I want a good 10 paces between you all. Let's go.' She took out her walkie talkie. 'Camp Lisa, this is Fox One. Three miles out. Mission a go, over.'

A crackle returned, with Grandpa's voice. 'Mission go, Fox One. Camp Lisa has your back. Over and out.'

Jack took a deep breath and fell into step behind Ade, who led the way.

Operation Underdog was officially underway.

Chapter 12

Two miles into their bleak march, trudging through fields, sweating from the efforts and the Texan heat, Jack spied a tumbleweed trundle by and chuckled, not believing he'd actually seen a tumbleweed outside of a Western movie.

When it fell, darkness was a relief from the heat.

The clear sky above them was like a studded blanket and the stars were joined by a waxing moon. It would be a week before it was full, Jack figured. Cooler the night might be, but more than once, he stumbled on rocks and dips in the ground.

After an hour of walking, a glow on the horizon became apparent and soon, unmistakable, tall narrow structures loomed.

The fuel facility.

Jack wet his lips and adjusted his grip on his rifle. The strap had slowly dug into his right shoulder, and his forearms ached from relieving it of the weight. Despite his talent for shooting, he'd never had to carry a fully loaded automatic rifle along with a laden backpack three-plus miles before.

He reminded himself that soldiers in the US military would have had to do this nearly every day and night, and his respect for them increased.

It wasn't just the backpack and guns that

weighed him down though, it was also the mental pressure of the task at hand. Now, with less than a mile to go, the fences to the facility slowly materializing out of the blackness and trees, Jack was fatigued and beginning to lose some of the energy and enthusiasm he'd had when they set out.

At the fence, Hailey moved left and crouched, waiting until the others, finishing with Jessie, who was bringing up the rear, had joined her. Dissatisfied with their spacing, Hailey raised her hand and gave them a sign to move in closer.

They followed the command quickly and quietly.

Hailey reached into her pack and withdrew wire cutters, making quick work of the hastily erected fence. It was clear the Chinese had built the complex hurriedly and perhaps with less care than if they'd had unlimited time.

Soon, she was able to pull the hole in the mesh wide enough for them to begin crawling through. Once they were all on the other side, Theo and Jack held the hole open for Hailey to pass through.

She gave the signal to spread out and crouch low in the grass to break up their shapes in the dark. Jack peered out across the facility; it was a sprawling scattering of low operational buildings, three large cylindrical fuel tanks, and a tall tower whose purpose was a mystery to him, with the structures connected via a complex array of pipes and feeds.

Truth be told, he had no idea how any of it worked. He'd never been to a fueling complex before. All he knew, was that this one had to be burned to the ground, one way or another.

Jack turned back quickly, so as not to miss Hailey's next signal.

This was it.

Her hand went up into the air and gave the go for them to fan out to their respective areas. With the map plans imprinted on his brain, Jack moved with his partner Murphy and approached the first building, crossing a stretch of hard ground.

To their left, Hailey and Ade went one way, and Theo and Jessie went another.

Holding up a hand, Jack motioned for Murphy to pause, while he checked out the side of the building they'd come to. There was no sight nor sound of the enemy. He gave the all-clear and they crept forward, hugging the edge of the building, navigating a few stacks of boxes, before reaching a back door.

Rising, Jack peeked through the small window to the side of the door. There were two Chinese soldiers inside, playing cards at a table. He ducked back down and gave the nod to Murphy, and they moved on.

Rifles at hand, but knives ready for their primary choice of attack, they padded quietly across another stretch of open ground, to the next building. Again, they check the windows, being careful they didn't get spotted, and in this building, Jack and Murphy saw a handful of officers conversing over some paperwork.

Odd, he thought. Everything seemed so calm, and they had yet to come across any armed guards. It was almost going too smoothly.

A few seconds later he had cause to curse himself for tempting fate. A guard appeared from the other building, strolling toward their location in the shadows. Jack and Murphy ran away from the building, ducking quickly behind a parked truck. With hearts pumping hard, they moved slowly to the rear to remain out of sight of the approaching soldier. Finally, he passed within just a few feet, and entered the officer's building via a side door.

'Jesus,' Jack mouthed to Murphy, whose eyes were wide with terror.

She shook her head in disbelief, then pointed ahead of them, toward the end of the long line of buildings where the set of tanks they were to place their charges on sat.

Jack nodded and they returned to the shadows, hugging the buildings in a crouched run as they headed towards the large tank. They had darted across another space and were on the move again when a door opened and a soldier stepped out into a pool of light, stopping them dead in their tracks.

The soldier's mouth dropped open, the cigarette he had been about to light up balancing precariously on his bottom lip.

The three stared at each other. Frozen, no one

reacted until a distant scream carried through the night air and jump-started them into action.

Hurriedly, Jack raised his rifle and squeezed the trigger but, so surprised had he been, he hadn't placed his feet correctly and the recoil sprayed his bullets into the side of the metal-clad building.

Swearing in Mandarin, the soldier scrambled for the pistol at his side but Murphy squeezed off a burst of fire that sent him clattering into the side of building then onto the ground, where he laid unmoving.

'Run!' screamed Murphy as shots of gunfire lit up the night.

Jack didn't have to be asked twice. Sticking to their original course, they sprinted towards the big cylindrical tanks. Glancing over his shoulder, Jack saw soldiers sprinting this way and that, already armed, almost as if they had been waiting for a disturbance.

There was a shout behind them, and a line of bullets stitched the wall to his left.

'In here!' Jack called, veering to the left amongst a forest of copper piping. They weaved their way deeper, putting copper pipes and vats between them and their pursuers, then veered towards their target.

The gunfire behind them ceased, the guards obviously concerned about a stray shot igniting the fuel around them. When Jack paused to see if they were being followed, he couldn't glimpse any Chinese uniforms amongst the pipes.

Catching his breath, he motioned to Murphy to take a sharp right and the pair ducked down behind some sort of unit, which offered them a bit of extra cover.

'There's no one there,' he said. 'We're not being followed.'

Murphy peered up over the unit, back the way they came, and Jack saw her blanch.

'We are,' she gasped. 'They're just not shooting! They're still coming in!'

'Shit!'

'What do we do? We can't shoot them, and they can't shoot us.'

Jack scrunched up his face. He knew what might have to happen.

'How many of them are there do you think? I counted four.'

'Same,' Murphy said.

'Shit!' Jack said. 'We're going to have to use these.'

He adjusted the strap on his rifle so that he could slip it onto his back, where it sat snug next to his backpack. Then he pulled out the long hunting knife by his side. Murphy stared at it, as if it was about to come alive and strike her.

'I was... I...' she stuttered. Fear taking grip.

'I don't want to either but...,' Jack said, his voice starting to shake, as the sound of hurried Mandarin floated over to their location—the soldiers nearing them with every step. 'We have no choice.'

'We could run for it? They can't shoot us, can they?'

'But they will,' he said. 'The second we leave this area.'

'Couldn't we...' Murphy's face contorted as she struggled to come up with an alternative to melee combat. 'Couldn't we run into the open and turn on them with our guns and blow the whole area up?'

'And us along with it,' Jack said. He held up the knife grimly and gripped it tight in his right fist. 'It's our only option.'

Murphy seemed on the verge of hyperventilating for a moment before she closed her eyes, reached for the knife and steadied herself. Jack watched in awe as she calmed and adjusted herself. Already, war had changed who they were.

In the Before Days, at this time of evening they would normally have been in a warm bedroom studying algebra or history, but instead, America had fallen, and they had seen war, death, and now were on the edge of their own demise.

The enemies' voices were close now.

Their time was up.

Jack held up three fingers and slowly counted them down, nodding to the left and right to indicate which way she should go. Murphy understood.

When he got to zero, he and Murphy sprang from either side of the unit, knives ready, and launched themselves at the unsuspecting soldiers.

Jack didn't allow himself to be distracted by what Murphy was doing. He was focused on his immediate target. Ahead, a tall soldier flinched at the unexpected movement but was barely able to swing his rifle more than an inch or two when Jack had tackled him, jamming his knife under his ribcage, driving it deep and holding the soldier in close until he stopped struggling. Blood gurgled from his mouth and down his chin as Jack gently laid him down.

Jack disengaged, his head pounding, adrenaline coursing through his body, and stood up to take stock of his surroundings. He spotted Murphy 20 feet away struggling with a soldier, blood splattering the ground. He didn't have time to ponder whose blood it was, because a third and fourth soldier tackled him to the ground in a tangle of limbs.

A fist struck Jack in the temple and light danced in his eyes as the knife was knocked from his hand.

No! He scrambled, fingers ferreting in the dirt, but couldn't find it. Instead, he found the groin of one of the soldiers and squeezed it with all his strength whilst taking a second blow from the other soldier, this time to the jaw.

The soldier's scream was high-pitched and the effect was immediate as he rolled away from them, clutching his groin. Unperturbed, the other soldier pinned Jack, wrapping his meaty hands around the boy's throat.

Static materialized on the edges of his vision as

he gasped for air and tried to pry the hand away from his throat. It was useless and he felt himself begin to lose consciousness.

With one last supreme effort, he reached around in the dirt for his knife and this time found the blade. Unmindful of the cut he inflicted in his palm when he gripped it, he pulled it to him and with numb fingers found the handle and drove it up under the chin of the Chinese soldier.

Blood poured from the wound, splattering Jack's face, seeping into his eyes and mouth.

The soldier convulsed and collapsed on him. With great effort, Jack rolled him over, exhausted, and stood up to see Murphy, sinking her blade into the chest of another soldier.

Murphy turned to Jack, saw the blood on him, then on her own hands and dropped the knife, shaking.

'I'm alright, it's his blood. What about you?'

Murphy touched a gash on her forehead.

'Just this... but oh my god Jack, I killed them-'

Jack grabbed her shoulders and looked at her.

'Don't let it sink in. Forget it. If you hadn't killed him, he would have killed you. Come on, we have to move. They know.'

'What?' she asked. 'What do they know?'

In the distance, they heard gunfire and more cries.

'This is an ambush,' he said. 'They knew we were coming.'

Chapter 13

Hailey was suspicious from the moment of her and Ade's first encounter.

Her Asian appearance caused confusion for the first soldier they ran into, and she took advantage of his hesitation, crossing the space between them and slicing his throat with a vicious flick before he could come to his senses. Ade had taken the second guard in a bear hug, snapping his neck with his powerful hands barely 30 seconds later, before a shot or scream had gone up.

They were stealthy and quick just like they had practiced, but the sudden appearance of a large number of soldiers from a group of buildings opposite the largest fuel tanks told her something wasn't right.

The invaders were expecting trouble, and this was almost certainly an ambush. A soldier screamed. They had been spotted.

'Run!' Hailey screamed at Ade, and she ran for a small building, throwing herself through the window as gunfire erupted behind them. Ade fell to the floor beside her, wincing as broken glass penetrated his shoulder and leg.

Inside, a surprised soldier shot to his feet and scrambled for a handgun on his desk. Hailey was on her feet almost preternaturally fast, and her throwing knife took him in the eye, causing him to fall back onto his chair, dead.

Hailey turned back to Ade as he struggled to his hands and knees, blood pouring from a wound on his leg, where a large shard of glass had lodged itself. He pulled it free and thankfully the blood didn't flow any faster. The gunfire had abated but the shouts of soldiers were coming closer.

'Stay down, and don't move,' said Hailey, crouching so she was below the window as she moved to the desk, where she freed her knife from its victim and proceeded to cut the sleeve of his uniform at the shoulder.

She went back to Ade and quickly and efficiently wrapped the material tight around his thigh.

'How is it?' she said, taking a peek through the broken window. The soldiers with guns were advancing. Five of them. 'Can you stand?'

'Yeah.'

'Good, because after we've dealt with these five, we will have to run to the first tank and place our charges. They know we're here, and we won't have much time. Do you think you can run on it?'

Ade gritted his jaw.

'Don't worry about me, I'll be fine.'

Hailey knew it hurt, but she also knew Ade was like a tank. When the time came he would push through the pain and do what he had to do.

Hailey motioned for him to take the other, smaller window on the far side of the office unit, while she flicked her rifle to automatic, and crawled to the broken window. Ade flicked off the lights as he went past the switch.

Good thinking, she thought.

More distant screams and gunfire lit up the night and Hailey knew the other teams had been engaged. Burying her concern, she placed the barrel of her weapon on the sill and carefully set her sights. The five soldiers had separated. Two on the left and three on the right, one group obviously intending to circle around and enter from the rear.

'No you don't,' she whispered, and gestured to Ade he should take care of the two on his side. He nodded. Hailey turned back and fired at the three who were closest to her. Her first volley took down the leading soldier, but the return fire was instantaneous and almost took her head off.

Ade followed suit from his side of the building, laying down fire.

He held up two fingers to Hailey, and she responded with one.

Three down. Two to go.

Gunfire continued for a full minute, peppering the building and sending glass and splinters of timber flying over her. Finally, it abated as the enemy reloaded and both Ade and Hailey opened up.

The remaining soldiers had taken cover behind a vehicle and when Ade and Hailey stopped to reload, they opened fire again.

'Shit!' she said. They were pinned.

They needed to try something before

reinforcements arrived.

Scuttling over to Ade, she whispered in his ear.

'Let off some fire, then scream, and slump back when they return. I will do the same. You crawl over to the door, I'll be lying under the window playing dead. When we have a shot, take it.'

Ade took the order and gave Hailey a thumbs up when she had made it back to her window. They began firing again.

After a burst of return fire, Ade let out a scream that would have done an Oscar winner proud and slumped to the floor. He was on the move immediately.

Hailey fired again for good measure, then also gave out a cry and ceased her firing as she rolled onto her front, her weapon outstretched but finger still on the trigger.

There were a few more sporadic bursts of fire before she heard harsh whispering close by and getting closer. It appeared they had taken the bait. With her heart beating hard, Hailey waited.

***

Theo placed the charge on a tank, right in the heart of the facility, whilst Jessie checked his flanks. Sweating, nervous from the sound of fighting all around them and knowing they had possibly been expected, he set the charges to blow in five minutes.

'Done,' he muttered.

They had just one more to do in their section

of the facility. Ambush or no, he and Jessie hadn't been spotted yet and with the work they'd done it would almost guarantee a chain-reaction, not allowing the Chinese time to disarm them even if they found them. Even one charge exploding would still cripple them enough to ruin the fueling operation for their Texas Command.

'You think it's a trap?' Jessie called back to Theo. 'The other teams have been engaged, but we came in so quietly...'

Theo let out a very slow, shaky breath as they hurriedly crossed the gap between the two large tanks.

'It's the only explanation,' he said, reaching the big smooth tank just ahead of her. 'But we need to focus on our task. The others will have to look after themselves. Cover me. I just have one left.'

'Hurry up,' she whispered. 'I get a feeling our luck might run out.'

He took the last charge from his backpack, knelt down by the tank wall, and placed the C4 up onto the cool metal exterior, pressing in on the sides to make sure it had stuck before he started to program the detonation sequence.

By the time he was done, his hands were shaking.

'Done,' he yelled. 'Let's get out of here and to the rendezvous— *SHIT*!'

A stray bullet flew by his head. Theo threw himself to the ground, biting his tongue as he rolled and feeling the coppery taste of blood fill his mouth.

Jessie spun around, ready to return fire.

'Don't fire, Jess!'

Her eyes widened as she realized the danger of a firefight so close to thousands of gallons of gasoline. She squatted next to Theo.

'We need to run for it,' said Theo. 'A stray bullet could light us up like the fourth of July.'

'Agreed. After three?'

'Fuck that,' he said, standing up. 'Go! Now!'

He leapt from his hiding spot and sprinted away from the tanks, with Jessie in tow.

Ahead of them, across open ground, they saw no cover. To their right, however, there was a small parking lot with a few trucks, cars and a van. All typical military, with the one exception a long dark sedan.

'There!' Theo screamed, flinching as bullets whizzed over their head as they fled across the yard. 'Head to the vehicles. Cover!'

Jessie's panting just behind him confirmed she was keeping up. Finally, they reached the parking lot and sprinted behind the first truck, skidding in the dry Texan dirt before hunkering down

They sheltered at one of the large rear wheels, so they wouldn't get picked off at the ankles. Shouts indicated the soldiers who had discovered them were hot on their tails. Theo dropped to his stomach and peered back the way they had come. Jessie watched as he moved his rifle into position and aimed it back under the truck. She followed suit at the rear of the wheel.

A burst from Theo's rifle took two down and a third soldier fell to Jessie's well-aimed shot to the head, but more appeared to replace them and their heavy fire had Theo and Jessie ducking back behind the wheels.

With their backs to the hard rubber of the tires, Theo spotted a pair of soldiers rounding a vehicle in the distance and heading their way, although they seemed to be unaware of their presence.

On a hair trigger, Theo fired at them without thinking, and cursed when he missed, succeeding only in alerting them.

'Fuck!'

The soldiers took cover and began to return fire.

'Shit!' Jessie screamed. 'We're screwed.'

'No,' he said. 'We got this.'

He raised his head, looking for the soldiers in front of them. A shot struck the tarpaulin side of the truck barely a foot above his head.

'I'll take care of those two, you go for the ones behind us, so we don't get flanked, got it?'

'Yes,' she said, reloading and chucking the empty magazine aside. She got back down and took aim under the truck.

Theo reloaded too and had barely raised his weapon when a harsh scream of Mandarin from a truck to the left told him the two soldiers that he'd engaged had split up.

A man with wild eyes wielding a handgun charged at Jessie, who was already firing her own weapon at the threat approaching from behind and totally unaware of the danger behind her.

'No!' Theo yelled, swinging his rifle around as the running soldier began shooting. He squeezed the trigger and watched the man jerk as his momentum was halted and he fell to the ground, dead. Jessie continued to fire under the truck, oblivious to the fact he'd just saved her life.

Unfortunately, Theo's attention had been occupied too long. The sound of running footsteps behind him told him he'd been bested. He waited for a hail of bullets in the back.

Sensing something was wrong, Jessie spotted the looming shadow behind Theo and quickly switched positions, raising her gun in her friend's direction. Understanding this was his only chance, Theo collapsed to the ground to give her an open shot but not before the soldier fired and he felt hot pain lance his back, just above his right hip.

He buried his face in the dirt as Jessie opened up, felling the man who shot him before she dropped to the ground and rolled, taking down another soldier who was rounding the truck before her gun clicked empty.

The last soldier poked his head around the corner as Jessie struggled to reload. Smiling, he emerged and aimed his weapon at her.

'You're fucked," he said in perfect English and squeezed his trigger. Nothing. He squeezed again, the smile slipping. When Jessie pulled out her pistol he slapped his open hand on his rifle frantically.

'Ni hao, mother fucker!' Jessie screamed and the soldier bucked twice as she emptied two bullets into his chest and skull.

Theo was impressed. Jessie had reached him before the man had even had a chance to fall to the ground. Swift as the wind she was at his side, pulling up his shirt and examining the wound on his front whilst he clenched his jaw to stop himself from crying out.

'Exit wound,' she said to him, eyes welling up. 'It's the exit wound. Thank god.'

'Yeah, got me in the back. I'll... aaah. I'll live, I think?' Theo managed to say, watching blood seep from the ugly wound. She pulled a thick wad of gauze from her small backpack and pushed it against the exit wound.

'Keep pressure on it with your hand. We have to move.'

With great difficulty, Jessie helped Theo up where he leaned unsteadily against her.

'How long do we have?' she asked, as they made their way across the parking lot, weaving between vehicles toward the rendezvous point.

Theo checked his watch and wished he hadn't.

Three minutes and 23 seconds.

'Shit...'

Chapter 14

Hailey heard footsteps just outside the window but forced herself to wait. Finally, she heard heavy breathing and a whisper of triumph. Simultaneously, her eyes snapped open, she raised the gun a few degrees and squeezed the trigger.

Ade had done the same.

The two Chinese soldiers jerked and spasmed under the onslaught, falling onto the ground, only one managing to let off a wild burst of fire as he collapsed. Hailey felt a sting on her right cheek.

'Yes!' rasped Ade.

Hailey wasted no time checking the wound and immediately climbed to her feet, offering her hand to him.

'No time to celebrate,' she said. 'Can you walk?'

Jack finished arming his charge, while Murphy finished with hers. Their timers were set to blow at the time they had all agreed to. The detour and fight had delayed them; they now only had two minutes. He stepped back, judging it to be secure, and raced across to Murphy.

The blood-soaked Murphy wiped her hands on her pants then set her timer.

'You good?'

Jack nodded.

'Done.'

From across the facility, a loud chorus of assault fire spurred them on. He prayed silently that the others would survive the onslaught and that they would escape without any further casualties.

Robert's dead face floated across his vision, only dissipating when Murphy shook him, her eyes full of concern.

'Jack, we can't afford to lose it now,' she said, her voice cracking.

'Sorry,' he replied, shaking his head. 'Do you remember the rendezvous point?'

'Yeah.'

'Good. Is your weapon fully loaded?'

Murphy gave him the thumbs up. Jack checked his again too.

'Come on,' he declared. 'Let's get home.'

With Jack leading, the pair slinked back through the pipe work from where they'd come, passing the dead enemy combatants, and paused only when they heard more gunfire.

Exchanging looks, they continued cautiously, glancing to their flanks and all around to make sure they weren't being snuck up on.

Someone knew they had planned to hit the facility tonight. Which meant that not only could more numbers be lurking, ready to make sure they didn't make it out alive, but that someone close to the camp, or within the camp itself, had leaked information to the Chinese.

A mole within Camp Lisa.

The thought churned in the acid of his gut. The

possibility of betrayal. It made him sick. Gripping his rifle tighter, he continued on.

Jack peered back down his iron sight, checking for movement, and briefly wished for night vision glasses. He froze when he spotted movement in the shadows of a long low building 30 yards away. Two figures, moving slowly.

One of them was limping. His wide frame was unmistakable.

Ade.

'Murphy,' he whispered and began to move forward. 'It's Hailey and Ade!'

Hailey spotted them at the same time and moved her hand urgently, almost frantically.

Not seeing the immediate danger, he hesitated and it almost cost him his life.

From behind the buildings at their rendezvous point 50 yards distant, a large group of the enemy emerged. There were dozens of them. Heavy gunfire erupted.

'Shit!' Murphy and Jack screamed in unison, throwing themselves behind a low wall, hitting the ground hard. Jack swore, feeling his right shoulder jar from the impact.

Bullets thunked into the cinderblock wall and whizzed over their heads. Jack crawled to the side and peered around carefully. Hailey and Ade had disappeared—hopefully into safety.

The cacophony of enemy fire made it hard for them to hear each other, but Murphy's shout finally reached his ears

'Where are the others? Can you see them?'

'I don't know!' he yelled back.

They were pinned now, blocked from escape. Jack slipped off his backpack, taking out the last magazines of ammo. Murphy did the same, their backpacks now significantly lighter with only basic medical supplies left in them.

Would they need to use them? Jack didn't think so. He wasn't sure they'd make another five minutes.

Jack held his weapon single-handed over the wall and shot off the last of the ammo. He then ejected the spent magazine and hammered home a fresh one, then sat back against the wall, feeling hopeless.

He blinked, then pictured Katie's face. Pictured the spot at the camp where he had fought his first group of Chinese soldiers. Remembered putting the first shovel full of soil on her grave.

His heart filled with new rage, and without telling Murphy of his intention, he stood up from the cover of the wall, a cry of anguish erupting from his throat as he fired at the enemy.

He didn't know how many he hit, or how close he came to dying, but he seemed to be shooting for an eternity, the rattle of his weapon shaking his body and the blazing muzzle flashes of the Chinese soldiers lighting up the night.

He was waiting for their bullets to put an end to him, but it was a sharp tug at his belt, pulling him downwards hard, that finally put him on the ground. Still in a frenzy, he turned his gun on Murphy who bravely slapped him across the cheek, snapping him out of his bloodlust.

'I'm sorry,' he whispered, putting his hand to his face. 'It's over Murph...'

***

Radio static burst from Jang Li's walkie talkie.

'Sir, we have engaged,' said the voice of his ground commander, gunfire in the background threatening to overwhelm his words.

'Perfect,' he replied. 'Make sure there are no survivors, and if even one of those charges goes off, it's your ass on the line, understand? Over.'

There was a pause punctuated by more shots.

'Understood Sir, over,' came the strained response.

Li put down the device and picked up a tumbler of American whiskey on ice he'd been nursing nervously for 20 minutes. He rolled the cool glass across his forehead before taking a gulp.

Through the door opposite, Lieutenant Wong emerged.

'Colonel,' he said, standing to attention and saluting.

Jang Li smirked.

'At ease.'

'Sir.' He relaxed, and gestured at the seat in front of Li's desk. 'May I?'

'You may,' Jang Li replied.

Wong settled down into the seat and the two

regarded each other. Jang Li raised his glass up and pointed to it with his other hand.

'I await an update that the survivors we ambushed, thanks to your intelligence gathering, are dead. When I do, I will pour you a glass. Do you know what it is?'

'No, Sir.'

'It's a 2013 Michter's Celebration Sour Mash Whiskey. It used to sell for thousands of dollars a bottle. I took this one from the Governor's mansion. It tastes like Yankee tears to me.'

'Yes Sir. I would be honored to try it.'

'Don't get ahead of yourself, there is some work for them to do before we celebrate.'

'Yes Sir. May I speak freely?'

'You may.'

'After this, what next? Camp Lisa?'

Jang Li smiled.

'Yes. You will snatch your informant and have him lead us to the enemy camp and we'll hang this leader, the old man, while they all watch.'

***

Having escaped the building and crossed a darkened path to a trailer, Hailey and Ade hunkered down in the shadow of a boiler. In the space between both ends of the building, she could see figures running. Lots of them, and they were armed to the teeth. They were trapped.

She put a hand to her cheek, and it came away smeared with blood. It had run in thick rivulets down her face and was seeping under her vest and shirt. She looked at Ade who, now that the adrenaline had worn off, looked as shocked at her appearance as she felt.

That stray bullet had been just an inch away from killing her.

Shaken by the near miss, she hunkered down next to him, and tried to collect her thoughts. Ade clutched his rifle close to his chest, and bowed his head, his lips moving without making a sound.

Hailey knew she'd remember this image. Of Ade, injured and bleeding in the dirt beside her, praying to survive the night. Shrugging off the backpack, she shuffled closer and gestured she was going to look at his wound.

He flinched as she parted the torn fabric of his pants. It was deep and dark blood pooled in the two inch-long slit, but it appeared to have stopped bleeding. She deftly unwrapped a bandaged and wrapped it tight around his thigh.

'I guess we're doomed, right?' Ade said, looking at her as she put her first aid kit back in the backpack.

His words hit her hard and she felt a lump rise in her throat.

'I'm sorry,' she said. 'I didn't...'

Ade's hand on her arm stunned her to silence.

'We did our best.'

'We did, didn't we? And we'll go out fighting, but first...' she paused and reached to the bottom of her pack. When she pulled her hand back out it was holding a military grade flare gun. She looked at him. 'I was hoping we wouldn't need to call on him, but we have to make sure this wasn't all for nothing.'

Ade nodded.

In one quick motion she put her arm straight up into the air and pulled the trigger. The blazing, hot-red comet soared through the night sky, searing a white line into her retinas as she watched it arc far over into the fields, away from sight.

As the excited voices of their hunters greeted the flare, there was no doubt in Hailey's mind that her father, who promised to be airborne for a full two hours during their mission, would see the signal.

She dropped the flare gun and picked up her rifle.

'Come on Ade.'

***

Theo muttered, angry at himself for letting the soldier get the drop on him. Hand on his side, he looked up at Jessie with tears in his eyes and apologized. With reinforcements coming from all directions, they had been forced to ground behind a bus.

'I've fucked it,' he said, pounding the ground.

'Don't be an ass,' Murphy shouted back to be heard. 'We aren't dead yet.'

'Look at me.'

'I am. And all I see is a baby bitching about a flesh

wound.'

Her scornful words cut through his self-pity better than a slap across the face may have.

She saw emotions war briefly on his face before finally, he burst out laughing. Jessie joined in, and for a brief moment of madness, they fell over each other, laughing hysterically.

Their mirth was interrupted by a bang and an incandescent glow in the sky. They broke away and followed the flare high into the night sky with their eyes.

'Hailey just called in Betsy…' said Jessie quietly. 'That means her and Ade are in trouble too.'

'So Grandpa is…'

'Yep. He's gonna light it up. They were hoping not to have to use the plane 'cos it's likely to trigger a last-ditch effort to weed out the camp. It's last resort, and she wouldn't have called him in if she didn't have to.'

His eyes widened.

'Which means, not only are the charges about to blow, but we also probably have Grandpa about to strafe us.' Almost as soon as he said it, they heard a distant whine like an angry mosquito.

'Well,' said Jessie, getting to her feet, throwing her spent rifle to the side and plucking her handgun from her belt. 'If we're gonna die in this shit hole, I'm taking a few out on the way. You with me?'

Theo winced as he struggled to a standing position beside her and slammed his last magazine home.

'You fucking bet.'

Chapter 15

By the light of the fading flare, Lieutenant Guo smirked, knowing they had the American scum pinned. Word had come in that all charges had been disarmed, and all that remained was for them to slowly close in on their positions and flush them out.

He reloaded his weapon and stood up before turning to his soldiers and ordering them to march forward. With their suppressing fire coming in short bursts, Guo was smiling from ear to ear.

Finally, after all the long years of training as a lowly private, he was getting to see the sort of serious action he'd been craving since he enlisted.

He held up a hand and his team stopped obediently. He wanted to tease this out and hang the promise of death in front of their eyes. It satisfied him to know that they were shaking in their boots and out of ammunition while death at the glorious hands of the People's Army inched their way.

He'd give it to them soon enough.

Satisfied that the fight was almost out of them, he motioned to the soldiers on either side of him to begin moving in closer to the buildings to flush them out. That was when he noticed a whining noise. It was faint and he almost dismissed it, but when he saw his men begin to look skyward, he knew he wasn't hearing things.

But no one was moving.

Guo cocked his head and stared to the heavens. The jet-black night, studded by bright stars, held barely a cloud. The noise grew louder.

A soldier three men down the line yelped, pointing into the distance just above the horizon.

Guo squinted as he struggled to spot what the man was pointing at. Then he saw it. Moonlight glinting off a sleek shape growing bigger by the second.

Realization dawned on him. It was a plane. An old one. In fact, it was a relic.

He laughed explosively and raised his gun but was beaten to the punch when what appeared to be fire erupted from its wings followed milliseconds later by the sound of machinegun fire.

'Run!' he screamed, but it was too late.

In swooped the aircraft, white hot metal cutting through the air and ripping up the ground, shredding his men to ribbons. He pushed one luckless soul out of the way and sprinted for the safety of a building 30 yards distant.

Then Guo tripped.

No! Not now, when I am so close to glory. Not now….

The hail of metal ended his thoughts as quickly as it shredded his body.

***

Above them, inside the cockpit, in his trusty leather pilot goggles, Grandpa gave a wave of his middle finger to the men he'd missed, who had scattered and were running in terror.

'Welcome to the neighborhood, assholes!'

He cackled wildly and banked, swinging around in a wide arc as he took more soldiers down. A second flyby was a risk, but he was willing to take it in order to allow as many of his people to escape as possible.

He was midway through cutting another swathe of men down when his ammo ran dry.

'Dang it!'

Just like that, he'd jinxed it.

To add insult to injury, a few stray bullets struck the underside of his plane, and the right wing. Betsy wobbled and he banked again only to have his attention drawn by a flash.

'Shit!'

It was small surface-to-air missile and it was heading straight for him.

He pulled the stick hard, pulling the protesting plane up at a sharp angle to avoid it.

'Come on Betsy,' he grunted. 'Don't fail me now!'

***

The distraction of her father's air raid and the subsequent panic of the soldiers gave Hailey and Ade the one shot they needed. Still supporting him, they managed to make it to the biggest of three circular tanks.

Ade covered her while she set charges on all three and set the timers for two minutes. It would have to be enough.

'We're done, come on Ade!'

As painful as the wound on his leg was, the thought of being blown to smithereens was enough to make Ade bury the pain and sprint for all he was worth, managing to just keep up with Hailey.

'Run!' Hailey screamed when she spied Jack and Murphy in the shadow of a building, watching a smoking Betsy just manage to avoid a missile and begin limping away from the arena.

Jack and Murphy didn't have to be told twice— while the soldiers were cowering under cover for the most part, this was the only chance they'd get to escape.

'Have you seen Theo and Jessie!?' Hailey panted as they sprinted for the fences.

'No,' said Jack. 'Should we go back for them?'

'No time! This motherfucker is about to blow…'

***

Theo and Jessie saw the soldiers scatter under Grandpa's unexpected aerial assault and Jessie immediately tried to tug him to his feet but Theo pulled away from her desperate grip.

'Come on Theo! We don't have time to fuck around.'

'I'm done Jessie,' he said, pointing down at his

belly. The exit wound was leaking blood profusely now and she could see from his pale features he was fading quickly.

'No! If we can get to the...'

'Jessie,' he said. 'I'm not gonna make it. It's bad.'

'Don't be a fu—'

'You need to go! Get to the rendezvous point. I'll hold them off.'

'Theo...'

Yelling and whooping broke out amongst the soldiers as Grandpa's plane gave up the fight and began to limp away, black smoke pouring from its engine.

There was a fresh pop of gunfire and Jessie looked over her shoulder. Theo took her hand and squeezed it and she looked back at him.

'You need to go. I'll hold them off so you can get clear.'

Jessie finally nodded, her eyes glinting with unshed tears. She didn't trust herself to speak, so settled for throwing her arms around him and kissing him on the cheek before hefting her gun and running off without a look back.

Theo's vision was blurred from tears too as he watched Jessie retreat. Not wasting any time, he buried his hand in his backpack and felt around until his fingers closed over a hard, round object.

The grenade was heavy in his left hand as he turned to face the sound of approaching soldiers. He pulled the pin and held the lever tight against the body of the deadly device as he used his other hand to pull out his Glock.

An excited yell went up and he knew he was spotted.

With all his remaining strength, he threw the grenade at the shapes rounding the corner of the big truck 20-feet distant. Excitement turned to panic and Theo began shooting.

The grenade exploded and those unlucky enough to be in the blast zone were blown to pieces. He managed to pick two more off before his Glock clicked empty.

He spied an enemy soldier peek cautiously around the corner where the pistol dangled in his hand. Theo gave him the finger and two Chinese-made bullets ended his life.

Jessie heard the small explosion and knew that Theo had just thrown his dingle grenade. A short volley of shots sounded then there was a silence followed by two in quick succession.

Jessie sobbed as she finally cleared the carpark and began running for the fences. That's when a large explosion lifted her off her feet like a gigantic, hot hand and threw her into the grass face first.

The explosion of the charges and the subsequent whump of the fuel igniting buffeted Hailey, Ade, Jack and Murphy but they managed to keep their feet. They finally made the fence and turned to watch in awe as the destruction of the three big tanks set off a chain reaction of smaller explosions.

'Let's get while the getting is good!' said Hailey.

'What about Theo and Jessie!?' asked Murphy.

'We can't wait here. They know the drill—if we're separated, they are to make their way to the farmhouse where we left the truck. We'll wait for them there. We only put ourselves at risk if we delay here.'

Murphy looked like she wanted to argue, but in the end, she simply nodded. She couldn't argue with the logic of the prearranged plan. None of them could.

'Come on.'

Chapter 16

The hike back to the farmhouse and truck was silent. Battered, bruised, and exhausted, and worried about the last two of their raiding party —Theo and Jessie—meant they were all lost in their own thoughts. Jack's concern was iced with a simmering anger that Hailey had not allowed them to wait.

While he knew from a tactical standpoint it was the right call, he didn't know how, as a human being, she could just cut them off.

They reached the barn three hours later, after having to interrupt their progress and pause numerous times to avoid several enemy choppers and their spotlights. They entered the barn and Hailey sat them down for a debrief.

'We wait here till an hour before dawn. The hour of darkness is all we need to get back to Camp.'

'What about Theo and Jessie?' asked Murphy.

'If they're not here, we have to assume the worst and leave. That was always the plan.'

'So, you're just going to leave them out to hang?' asked Jack bitterly.

'They knew the risk!' snapped Hailey, a glimpse of her true emotions breaching the surface of her cool demeanor before she put a lid on them. 'We all did.'

Murphy put a comforting hand on her shoulder and Jack left another bitter retort unsaid.

'I want everyone to get some rest. I'll keep watch,' said Hailey, standing up and walking away.

Jack's body ached and his ears were still ringing from the blast. He climbed into the flatbed with the others, his throat so dry from smoke inhalation that it was an effort just to swallow. He greedily finished one of the water canisters.

He joined the others, who had bunched up their packs and were resting their heads on the makeshift pillows. He looked up at the darkened barn ceiling, thinking there was no way he could sleep. But exhaustion overtook his body, and he did.

***

Jack awoke to the sound of harsh whispering.

With his heart humping hard in his chest, he snapped to attention and spied Hailey at the gap between the big doors of the barn; Ade was behind her, gun in hand.

On full alert, Jack grabbed his pistol and jumped down from the truck, running across to Hailey and Ade.

Before he reached them, Hailey made a noise deep in her throat and reefed the door open before running out into the darkness.

Ade looked over his shoulder at Jack.

'It's Jessie!' he said and followed their leader out.

Jack dashed through the doors after him and

they found Hailey about 30 feet away, holding a limping Jessie upright and helping her towards the barn.

The young girl was pale and dirty, and she was clearly injured. She gave the boys a pained smile as they crowded around.

'Give her space,' said Hailey. 'I've got her. Jack, get a blanket set up on the floor and Ade, grab the big first aid kit from the truck cabin.'

An hour later, Hailey had treated Jessie's wounds. She had taken some shrapnel from the explosions in the shoulder and just above her right buttock, and also had abrasions on her hands and knees.

Hailey had managed to remove the small piece of shrapnel from her shoulder, but the other was deeper and would need to be removed when they were back at camp where she had more appropriate instruments. She had cleaned all of her wounds with alcohol and bandaged them well enough to last the trip home.

Hailey shushed Jessie when she tried to talk about what happened to Theo.

'It's okay hun, rest for now, you're going to need all your strength. We'll talk about it all when we get back to camp.'

The faint light of dawn was in the east by the time Hailey finished. They backed the truck out of the barn for the run back to camp.

When the crunch of stone and mud under the

tires changed to the smooth hum of asphalt, they all turned their heads south, toward Houston, the light of dawn displaying the thick smoke in the distance, still billowing like a volcanic eruption, filling the sky and turning the dawn red.

It bled right across the horizon, and an old rhyme came to Jack then. Something his Dad used to say years ago, usually with his hands on his hips, staring out through the kitchen window into the distance.

'Red sky in the morning, a shepherd's warning.'

Jack thought it fitting.

He cast his mind back to the fighting, and what they knew now to be the ambush. Someone had given the heads up, and that could only mean one thing.

They had a mole in the camp.

Watching the ribbon of road peel away from them as the sun slowly climbed into the heavens, Jack tried to consider what it would take for an American to betray their country. To betray their own people—what was now akin to *family*.

Camp Lisa wasn't just a guerilla camp or a rebel base. It had become a home. A place where everyone had become the proxy family they all craved, after losing everyone else when the virus had swept across the continent.

So who was the betrayer?

Gripping the side of the truck, now halfway to the forest, Jack adjusted his position and gritted his teeth. He had a new objective. A single objective once they got back. He would find the mole. And he would kill them.

***

'What do you mean, they've escaped? We had them cornered! We ambushed them!'

Wong roared with frustration, throwing his hat at the private who stood before him—one of few who had survived the attack at the fueling facility north of the city.

He took stock of the private's left arm in a sling, the cuts on his face and singed hair, and wished it had been worse.

Private Xi Lang shuffled uncomfortably and made to pick up the hat. This only enraged Wong further, who kicked at his hand and ordered him to stand to attention.

'Tell me what happened, with no bullshit or I swear I'll shoot you where you stand,' he roared.

He asked, but the Lieutenant knew perfectly what had happened. Word had reached him shortly after the fighting had started, and he had expected an update in short order to inform him of success.

That went out of the window, literally, when enormous explosions had lit up the night. From the big window of his office in Houston's Texas Command it played out in glorious color, signaling that the rebels had somehow, against all odds, achieved their objective.

Word from Jang Li's office had reached him and,

apparently, he was not pleased. In fact, he was murderous. That meant Wong's head was on Jang Li's chopping block. And Li's in turn would be facing scrutiny from above. Shit didn't hit the fan in the Red Army, it fell down from above.

A scapegoat was required.

Wong stomped his feet when the private hesitated to respond.

'Speak!'

'S-sorry, Sir. We... we had the advantage—'

Wong slapped him hard across the face.

'Do. Not. Lie. To. Me.'

The private yelped, his eyes bulged in shock.

Wong raised his hand again to strike him.

'No! I'll tell you!' Xi Lang cried.

'Go on.'

'Reinforcements. We didn't have intel about them.'

'Reinforcements?' Wong asked, feigning the confusion that would someone hearing of it for the first time would show. Because, of course, he knew.

'Yes, Sir. Reinforcements. An old American plane. Almost certainly the same one seen in Huntsville earlier this year. I'm almost sure of that, Sir.' He took a breath. 'It came from the north, keeping low to the ground. We didn't see it until it was too late. We eventually returned fire and damaged it but in the meantime the infiltrators must have had time to plant more charges.'

Wong slapped him again.

'Liar! You say no survivors and yet here you are, like a turd on legs, stinking out my office. Correct your story, Private.'

'Sorry, Sir. I was on high ground, Sir. Further to the outskirts of the facility. I managed, in fact, to damage the plane.'

Private Xi Lang mistook the look on Wong's face to be one of approval. It was, in fact, awe that the private would take credit for allowing the enemy to escape.

Big mistake.

'Oh?'

'Yes, Sir. I shot at the traitor and damaged the aircraft.'

'And did it come down?'

'…No, Sir.'

'Did it, perhaps, land further away due to damage?'

Xi Lang started to fidget with his sling, knowing, somehow, he had said something gravely wrong.

'No, it didn't, Sir, but—'

'So,' Wong interrupted, his voice raising, hoping he had channeled enough of the terrifying persona of Colonel Jang Li. 'He is not dead and was also able to escape, and with your failure, it allowed the other survivors to escape?'

Lang looked like a trapped animal. He saw no way out and lowered his head.

'Yes, Sir.'

Wong struck the soldier twice with the back of

his hand, first left then right hand.

'Incompetence! You are almost solely responsible for the destruction of the facility AND allowing the rebels to escape!'

Cowering, the private yelled desperately.

'No... Sir!'

Wong's eyes bulged, shaking with rage now. 'What?'

'One of them died. He detonated himself and killed many comrades, it allowed his partner to escape just as the charges began exploding.'

'This does not mitigate your incompetence! You will be placed into custody and shortly be required to sign a statement admitting full responsibility for the destruction of the facility and the escape of nearly all the terrorists. Guard!'

'Please Sir, I—'

'Get him out of my sight!' snapped Wong when the military guard entered. 'Solitary confinement —no contact with anyone.'

'Yes Sir!'

When the door closed, Wong circled back behind his desk and sat down before tapping the space bar to wake up his computer. He had his scapegoat, he just had to hope that Colonel Li would accept Xi Lang's confession.

He began typing.

I, Private Xi Lang, hereby state that the following is a true account of the events...

PART 3: THE MOLE

Chapter 17

Branches whipped the side of the truck. The morning sun was now high in the sky and the survivors, covered in dirt, blood and ash, stared longingly at the overgrown track ahead as the truck neared its destination.

When they finally arrived at the clearing at the southern edge of camp, their campmates came pouring out from the tents and shelters. Before she could even turn off the vehicle, their people, followed closely by a frantic grandpa, were moving in and around the weary survivors as they climbed down, covering the truck with loose branches and grass to camouflage it.

'Where's Hailey?!' Grandpa shouted, pushing people out of the way.

The tone of his plaintive call cut though Jack. It was unadulterated fear.

'I'm here, old man,' she said, ducking under a tall kid throwing a branch over the top of the truck's cabin.

Grandpa fumbled past everyone and ran into his daughter's arms.

'Thank God!' he breathed as they embraced. The old man wore his heart on his sleeve and Jack caught the unmistakable sob of relief, but he was more surprised at the tears he saw in Hailey's eyes.

He watched them, thinking of his own parents for the first time in a long time. He wiped a tear from his own eye.

When they broke apart, Grandpa looked around at the others in the party, clearly counting heads before looking at Hailey sharply.

'Theo?'

Hailey shook her head, clearly not trusting herself to speak.

'Oh no, poor Theo…'

'Okay!' called Hailey, suddenly all business again. 'Finish covering the truck. Jack and Ade, go to the medical tent for treatment. Murphy, please organize a stretcher for Jessie and stay with her when they bring her down, while I go with Grandpa and the boys to get things ready.'

Grandpa went to Jessie, who had been helped down from the truck and was resting in the shade of a tree with Murphy at her side. His eyes were pained as he looked her over.

'We'll get you right as rain young Jessie. Just relax here till they bring you down.'

Jack turned to follow Grandpa when he got back up; Hailey and Ade had already set off. From the corner of his eye, he saw movement in the people that had gathered and turned to see Jen nudging her way through the crowd. He stopped and waited for her, unsure how to greet her given their recent history. He didn't have to worry—while he smiled and raised a hand awkwardly, she walked right up to him and took him in a bear hug.

'Thank God you're okay. Is everyone back safe this time?'

Jack's brain froze at the question. How was he to break the news that they had lost someone else? Thankfully, Grandpa came to his rescue, swiveling and putting a hand on Jen's shoulder as she and Jack separated.

'Jen, we lost Theo…'

'No!'

It wasn't Jen who screamed, in fact she took the news stoically and instead turned her concerned eyes on Ruby, the red-haired survivor who had screamed the denial, and was now bent over double as grief took ahold of her.

'Theo died saving us,' Jack announced, in a solemn voice loud enough for all to hear as Jen went to the girl. 'He died to save us. He died a hero.'

'It's true,' Jessie said, weakly as she was lifted onto the stretcher. 'He made me promise to run… and he…'

'No…' Ruby said, hand to her mouth.

The other onlookers all looked shocked, and Jack had to admit, if one of them wasn't going to make it back alive, he wouldn't have picked Theo to be the one.

'What happened? I thought it was a stealth mission. Did… did something go wrong?' Bradley, one of the younger kids, piped up.

Murphy put a supportive arm around Jessie, almost as if to shield her from any more questions.

'Enough questions,' Jack said. 'There'll be a

debrief later, clear the way so we can get Jessie to triage.'

***

Hailey stretched the kinks from her back as she breathed in the cool night air. It had been a long day, but it was done now, and she was done too.

The survivors had all been seen to, and the worst of them, Jessie, was resting comfortably, the shrapnel that had been lodged deep in the flesh of her buttock removed and the wound stitched. She was young and her physical injuries would heal quickly. The mental ones might take a little longer.

Fatigued and aching from head to toe, Hailey collapsed into an old deckchair in the corner, praying it wouldn't buckle and spill her onto the floor today of all days.

Rubbing her face with her hands, she leaned forward into and slowly worked at her eyes with the edges of her palms, as she finally began to fully process the events of the last 24 hours.

They had a rat in camp, that much was clear. The Chinese could be just hours behind them. They needed a plan, but her mind was a wild mess.

Letting out a long groan, she looked up at the ceiling of the tent and closed her eyes.

Someone close by cleared their throat and she opened her eyes. A familiar, silhouetted figure stood in the open doorway of the tent.

'Honey,' Grandpa said. 'How are you feeling?'

'Horrible,' she grumbled. 'How's old Betsy?'

'In bad shape, but nothing a little elbow grease can't fix.'

'I could do with some of that elbow grease. And a drink,' she said, struggling out of the chair. 'But first I need to clean myself up. Can you see a towel anywhere?'

Grandpa looked to the left, leaned into a clear plastic box and pulled out a fresh towel. 'Here you go, honey. And after you clean up, I want you in bed, you hear? You're no good to anyone if you're too tired to speak.'

Hailey smiled. He knew her too well. They were peas in a pod. The old man had given her not just her genes but had shaped so much of her life and her ways of thinking and coping with problems.

He'd always been the one that helped her keep her fortitude in that grey zone between the culture of her American mother and Chinese father. She was an American, but of course, occasionally the 1% got through her defenses with a remark here or there. *You speak such good English! Where are you from?*

Generally, those people, she was sure, meant no harm. There were worse. Much worse, but they were few and far between.

Now none of it mattered. There was no America anymore. They were all just *survivors* now. Although she was sure the invaders would judge them as traitors.

Mom would have been so proud of him... but what would she have made of me losing two kids in as many weeks?

As if hearing her thoughts, he stepped forward, put a hand on her arm and shook his head.

'I want you to get rid of those demons in your head. You hear me, kid? You're a fighter, and you did what you had to do. Your mother would have understood that, too. This was war.'

'I know, Dad, but…'

'Don't lose your fighting spirit. You're our strongest and we need it. The enemy is out there, and they'll spend every waking moment trying to extinguish it. You fight for you, and you'll be strong enough to fight for us.'

She smiled and wiped a tear away from her eye.

'Always the way with words, Dad. Don't worry, they haven't knocked the fight out of me yet.'

'Good,' he said. 'That's my girl. Now, go get washed up and I'll bring you that drink to help you get off to sleep. I'll take care of this family of ours tonight. We ain't done living yet.'

'No,' Hailey nodded, tucking the towel under her arm, and following him through the door. 'No, we're not.'

***

The next morning Jack left camp early and headed to the lake for some alone time. When he got there, he sat down in the tall grass, watching the wind chop at the lake's surface and enjoyed the cooling breeze of another hot summer's day.

It felt weird to be back in his spot. The last time

he'd been here, Robert and Theo were still alive, and a chirpy Jen had come to find him and bring him back to camp. In the process, she had lifted his spirits immeasurably.

Something told him Jen wouldn't be looking for him this time and though he'd ventured out from the camp for solitude, a small part of him wanted someone to come out to comfort him.

After an hour in the sun, he went back into the shade of a large oak tree. Despite growing up in California, he still burned easily. He'd burn red then fade back to his usual pale within days. His sister Katie, on the other hand, would always tan and Dad would always joke that she'd got the mailman's genes.

Jack bowed his head, as the grief over his lost family unexpectedly overwhelmed him and tears spilled onto his jeans.

He tried to drive it away, but that only opened up a vivid slideshow of all the people he'd killed. Larry Dawson, the pervert neighbor. The soldiers who had attacked Katie. The female soldier who'd surprised him at the school. All the others in Sacramento. Huntsville. Coldspring... and the latest at the fuel facility.

A chorus of gun fire and screams played as a soundtrack.

Eventually he knew the only way to silence the noise in his head was to get up and get moving, so he headed back to camp. The walk was uneventful and seemed twice as long as the first leg.

When he got back to Camp Lisa, everyone seemed to be busy doing something and he felt a tinge of guilt at going MIA.

He waved at Ruby as he walked by but only got a sharp nod in return as the eyes of other kids around her followed him. The same again when he passed the group working on that night's meal. Some of the glances were downright hostile.

What's up with that? He asked himself.

He passed Ade coming from the trenches with a bag of potatoes.

'Hey Ade, is everything okay?'

'Where have you been?' Ade said quietly, putting the potatoes down and stepping in close.

'I… I just went for a walk, to clear my head. Why what's happening?'

'Man, you need to make sure you clear it with Hailey next time. The rumor about the mole is out and people are getting paranoid. You disappearing like that has tongues wagging.'

Jack frowned.

'What!?' Jack hissed. 'I'm not the fucking mole! I was there, remember?!'

Ade gestured for him to keep his voice down and looked around.

'Jack, you don't have to convince me of shit, but you know how rumors can spread, so just go and speak with Hailey and Gramps, quick.'

'God damn it,' Jack said, shaking his head, and feeling a deep sense of betrayal in his guts.

'I know. The sooner we find this mole and take

care of them, the better.'

Chapter 18

So angry was Jack from his campmates' suspicion that he went straight to his tent. As far as he was concerned, they could all go to hell. How could they even think that he was the traitor? The idea was so stupid it incensed him.

As soon as he was lying down on his bedroll though, the exhaustion overtook him, and not even the seething anger could prevent him from closing his eyes. He fell into a fitful sleep.

He wasn't sure how long he was out, but when he awoke from his heavy sleep, dazed and confused, the light of the day was fading, and he was hot and sweaty from the humidity in the zipped-up tent.

He groaned as he rolled off his bedroll and stood up. His anger had subsided somewhat and as he pulled his sweaty shirt away from his armpit and sniffed, he decided he would wash up before he went to see Hailey and Grandpa.

Grabbing his towel and the sliver of soap he had left, he ducked through the tent flaps and headed for the showers. He'd barely taken two paces when somebody's arm wrapped itself around his throat from behind and dragged him backwards as a second figure, wearing a mask and hoodie, lunged toward him and sunk a fist into his belly.

The air was expelled from his lungs in an explosive gasp and Jack sagged against the person who had accosted him from behind. Dazed, he put his hands up to the arm around his neck.

'Fucking rat!' spat the guy in front of him, and swung again, this time connecting it with his jaw.

Seeing stars but knowing the guy would wind up for another punch any second, Jack lifted his feet and let the guy behind take his full weight, dragging him over enough until he let go, causing the assailant's next punch to hit his own guy in the face.

Jack then lashed out with his foot and took the puncher in the groin. That was enough for the cowards, who, swearing and groaning in pain, sprinted off as Jack rolled over and tried to get his breath back.

Jack looked after them, but in the twilight and wearing hoodies there was no way to tell for sure who they were, although the one clutching his groin was built a lot like Bradley, a 15-year-old kid who, up until now at least, he liked and had gotten along with really well.

Feeling more emotionally hurt than injured, he picked himself up, dusted himself off and headed for the washroom.

He was almost there when Grandpa rounded the corner of a distant tent.

'Ahh, Jack, I was just coming to see you... what happened?' the old man said when he saw Jack's bruised cheek.

'Hey, Grandpa,' he coughed. 'Nothing. I'm okay.'

'"Nothing" doesn't leave a bruise like that.'

Jack shook his head.

'It was just a misunderstanding.'

'Tell me who did this. I won't have dissent in this camp—'

'Grandpa. It's nothing, and I didn't see who it was.' Jack winced when Grandpa reached out to touch his cheek gently. 'They're just looking for someone to blame and I'm the obvious choice for being the rat because I haven't been here as long and because I like to wander off.'

'Well, I won't have vigilantes roaming the camp. Hailey and I are figuring it out, until then, life will go on as normal.'

Jack gestured to his face.

'Seems everyone else wants to find the rat too.'

'I'm sorry, kid. Really, I am. I'll make an announcement at dinner, but in the meantime, I have an idea that will keep you busy and outside the camp until things blow over. Like the sound of that?'

'Yeah,' he said. 'That's exactly what I need right now.'

'Good, because I sure could use your help getting Betsy fighting fit...'

They arranged to meet at the truck the next morning at 6am. The evening meal had been hell for Jack; every time he caught someone looking his way, he was paranoid they were thinking he was the rat.

The big smile Jen gave him when she sat down opposite him for dessert warmed him. If Jen had looked at him with suspicion, it would have been the last straw. With her and Grandpa and Hailey on his side, he could deal with the misguided distrust of the rest of the camp.

It was nice waking up and walking through camp while everyone else was asleep. Grandpa was already at the truck, uncovering it after topping up the fuel with a jerrycan.

'You sure we shouldn't walk?' Jack asked. 'In case the truck is spotted from the air?'

Grandpa laughed.

'You can walk if you want kid, but it's a little too far for my old legs.'

Jack had never been given the privilege of seeing Betsy, or where exactly she was stationed. It was a closely guarded secret between Grandpa and Hailey and maybe two of Jack's campmates. He suspected that was mainly because the old man occasionally needed his own space, a man cave of sorts, but also because it was possibly the most vital piece of self defense weaponry they had.

Now their caution in keeping its location secret turned out to be absolutely the right call and Jack knew he didn't have to worry about the two camp leaders doubting his trustworthiness if he was being let in on the secret.

When Grandpa turned the truck about and left Camp Lisa, they headed deeper into the forest, rather than out toward open ground, which is what Jack was expecting him to do.

Trees whipped at the side of the truck and, hanging on the rearview mirror, a set of prayer beads wobbled back and forth in time with the bouncing of the truck, threatening to fly off on particularly violent turns and bumps.

Grandpa had told him in his first month at camp that his dead wife had been a staunch Roman Catholic. When she had passed, in the fighting, Grandpa had vowed to carry it with him everywhere he went.

After 15 minutes of driving, they came to an abrupt stop in the very heart of the national park.

'From here we go on foot, kid.'

Jack climbed out and peered around. The road they'd travelled was barely recognizable as an off-road track but they were in a flattened area now, ringed on the edges by cut tree branches and trunks.

'Come on now, this way,' he grumbled, rolling his denim shirt sleeves to the elbows. Jack was glad he'd worn his hiking boots as he followed Grandpa into an opening in the undergrowth.

***

Back at camp, Hailey waved to Ade and Murphy who pulled the crudely built timber structure trap to the edge of the big freshly dug hole on the outskirts of camp. With ropes they lowered it into the hole and once in place, they covered it with a net and kicked leaves and sticks over it to camouflage it.

'Careful you don't lose your balance,' said Hailey.

Crude it might be, but the six sharpened stakes protruding from the top would be a deadly welcome for anyone who fell in—hopefully an enemy soldier.

Elsewhere around the wide perimeter of Camp Lisa, Hailey acted as operations director, pointing and ordering small groups she had organized into setting up various wire trips and other traps hidden in holes.

Tonight, when they were all laid, she would take groups of the campmates around until they had all committed the locations of the traps to memory.

A hundred yards out from the perimeter of camp, they set up tripwires strung between trees at shin height. The end of each tripwire went into a contraption they nailed to a tree, out of sight.

Hailey knelt down into the mud and pointed to the last one they had rigged to go. Ruby looked curious, combing her sweaty red hair behind her ears and frowning.

'Wanna see how this works?'

'Yeah,' she said, fascinated. 'I don't get how you

fire a bullet without a gun.'

Hailey smiled, adjusting the bandana that was tied over her forehead, keeping her hair back.

'Right, well, these aren't bullets, they are shotgun shells, but do you know what makes a bullet shot from a gun?'

'Trigger'

'Not quite. To keep it basic, there's a whole bunch of pins and springs inside a gun, and in essence, when you pull the trigger, it makes the hammer slam home into a firing pin, which is like a spring behind the bullet. That firing pin hits the primer, which causes an explosion, which ignites the gunpowder within the cartridge. All the expanding gas from that, inside the chamber —'

'—that's happening all inside the gun's chamber?' Ruby gawked, mouth falling open.

Hailey laughed. 'Sure is. And *boom*, that's how a bullet flies out so fast, and why the chamber releases and an empty cartridge is spelled. That's why you kids have to clean up all those *bits of metal*, as you call them.'

'Ahh okay. So, is that how this trap is meant to work?'

Hailey nodded. 'Similar, yes. Same principle. When someone trips the wire, it's connected to this bit here, which is attached to the mousetrap doohickey, and it snaps shut, creating that hammer and pin impact, and *boom*.'

Ruby stuck her tongue out in concentration,

looking back and forth between the trip wire and the trap components on the tree.

'Will it hit them and kill them?'

'No, these are shotgun shells, so they'll explode, and it'll be loud but there'll be limited damage. It'll be enough for what we want it to do though, which is sound an alarm and give us time to prepare. But, if we're lucky, one maybe two soldiers might find themselves with a nice big hole blown through their legs.'

'Amazing. Wow, I always learn so much from you Hailey. These lessons of yours sure beats calculus.'

Hailey frowned as the pair both stood, brushing off the dirt and leaves.

'You don't miss school? Not a bit?'

A shadow of the past flitted across Ruby's face. Briefly. Then it was gone.

'I think I used to.' She shrugged. 'But that's all gone now.'

***

Finally emerging from the trees after a difficult walk through the thick scrub, Jack was surprised to find a long stretch of open road, wide enough for a lane of traffic in each direction. Toward the end of it, he could make out two small holiday cabins, and to the right, a cabin with its own large garage. And perfect size, too, judging by the home DIY modifications that had been made to it since.

Jack grinned.

'Guess you got busy and made it a home for Betsy, right?'

Grandpa winked. 'Damn right, kid. Keeps her out of sight, too. This piece of road was meant to link in, I think, but work was never finished. It's a dead end, and the cabins here are all unoccupied, most not even fitted with plumbing or electrics.'

'Right,' he said, following Grandpa over to the large garage, whose door had been removed and widened to allow space for Betsy to taxi in and out.

'Hang on,' Jack said, wiping some sweat from his brow. 'If there's no electricity, how do you work on Betsy?'

'Old fashioned way. Nails and hammers.'

Jack's face fell.

'What?'

Grandpa barked out a loud laugh that echoed into the trees, frightening a few birds into flight. He slapped Jack on the shoulder and ushered him into the garage. 'I'm just messin' with ya, kid. I found an old generator, which runs on gas. I use it sparingly, as we need reserves to run the trucks, but it doesn't use much.'

After Jack's eyes adjusted to the poor light inside the garage, he marveled at the World War 2 era plane, up close and personal. Aside from the damage from the recent encounter, it was a thing of beauty.

Behind the plane sat rows of equipment, tools and other items.

'Where should I begin?'

Grandpa winked at him, walked over to a large box and pulled open the lid. Inside were thin pieces of sheet metal. He then pointed to a workbench on the opposite side, next to which stood a big tank attached to what looked like a welding tool.

'Ever used one of those?'

Jack shook his head.

'Well, you're about to.'

Chapter 19

Grandpa's trust of Jack seemed to ease some of the tension in camp, but Jack was more than happy to be off site and working with Grandpa during the day.

They had worked late into the night on the first day and had left camp again early the next morning. On a break the second day, it dawned on Jack that he hadn't even asked the old man where he'd gotten Betsy.

'Well, kid,' he said, lighting a cigarette from a secret stash he had in the workshop. 'I wasn't joking when I said it was a museum piece. But a working one at that. When I returned from commercial flying, I joined a flight club. It was just a bunch of like-minded old boys that liked to tinker with beauties like this and, of course, fly them. When the virus hit at Christmas and I found out who was responsible, I went to the airfield and collected Betsy first thing.'

'Who named her Betsy? Was it you?'

'It was,' he said. 'Named after my first girlfriend —don't go telling Hailey that though!'

Jack laughed. 'I won't.'

After another few hours, they packed it up and headed back to camp.

***

After two full days, Betsy was patched and repaired to Grandpa's satisfaction.

It looked pretty rough to Jack, but the old man assured him it didn't need to be a work of art.

'The damage was only on the fuselage, none of the machinery or the wings or I wouldn't be here talking about it most likely.' He rubbed the plane's flank fondly. 'I think scars are sexy, don't you? Come, we'll fill her up and kick her over.'

Grandpa stepped up the ladder and squeezed himself into the cockpit.

'Come on up!'

Placing the toolkit down onto the workbench, Jack clambered up and stood on the wing, staring at the instrument panel.

'Wow,' he whispered, looking at the confusing array of dials, switches and gauges. 'Looks confusing.'

'Not as complicated as you think,' said Grandpa. The old man proceeded to give him a brief explanation of the instruments. 'See?'

'Nope,' said Jack. 'Still confusing.'

Grandpa chortled.

'Okay, son. Hop down and go out front so you don't get blown over.'

When Jack was safely outside, Grandpa kicked the engine over. It coughed and spluttered but didn't start. It did the same on the second try. Grandpa swore after the third attempt and reached out and slapped the side of the plane.

The engines roared to life on the fourth attempt and Jack whooped when Grandpa gave him the thumbs up. The noise and smell of gasoline was overwhelming.

Grandpa let it run for a few minutes then switched it off. Once he'd climbed down, they put the rest of their tools away and he put his arm around Jack's shoulders on the way through the door.

'Good job son, couldn't have done without you.'

Right then, Jack was the happiest he'd been since America fell.

By the time they got back to the newly fortified camp, it was dark, and dinner was being served up. Jack was starving and was gratified that Murphy was in charge of the cooking. She was without a doubt the best of all of them, and the venison stew smelled delicious.

Jack still had the feeling he was being watched with suspicion by a handful of the campmates, but the people that really mattered—Murphy, Ade, Hailey, a quickly recovering Jessie and, of course, Grandpa—made a special effort to include him and loudly reinforce their trust.

The only other opinion he cared about was Jen's. She was sitting across and three seats down from him and seemed withdrawn and solemn, but he didn't think it had anything to do with whatever gossip might be doing the rounds about him.

Robert's death had changed her, but Theo's

death so soon after seemed to have really nailed home just how tenuous their hold on safety and security was. He had a feeling she was suffering from depression and made a promise to himself to speak to her later.

The talk at the table was almost non-existent. Hailey had been working everyone hard to fortify their defenses and prepare for an attack they all felt was inevitable.

The silence was broken when on the other table Bradley muttered something to Todd, who was across from him.

'Huh?' asked Todd.

'I said, what did your mom have to say today? You know, when you disappeared again?'

Todd reddened and bowed his head, staring down into his bowl of stew.

'She doesn't talk to me, I talk to her.'

'Damn. Nothing?'

'No.'

'Come on, Bradley,' Jessie snapped. 'Give the kid a break. What he talks about to her is his business.'

'Baby...' Bradley said.

Todd pushed his bowl away and got up, his face red with embarrassment. He left the mess tent without looking back. Whispering broke out amongst the other diners and Jack spotted Grandpa squeeze Hailey's hand when she made to stand up.

Bradley sneered and looked around, his eyes falling on Jack.

'Something to say, Rat?'

'Hey!' Grandpa shouted, making quite a few of the kids jump. 'No bullshit allegations until we get to the bottom of it, you got it?'

No response.

'I said, have you got it?'

'Yes, Sir,' Bradley said, throwing Jack a baleful last glance before turning back to his stew.

***

Colonel Jang Li, in his perfectly pressed uniform, walked with Wong down one of the main thoroughfares in the city of Houston.

A strong, cool wind whipped between the towering skyscrapers and buffeted them. Wong shivered, but it had nothing to do with the chill in the air. He had barely managed to survive the debacle at the fuel facility, only saving his ass when offering up the scalp of the lowly private Xi Lang.

'Lieutenant, you find yourself delivering this news at a very, very convenient time. General Hao will be arriving tomorrow morning for a conference with Texas Command. He will be pleased when you deliver the perpetrators of the horrendous crime against his daughter. I have informed him that you, yourself, will be leading the mission. Of course, if you fail...'

Colonel Jang Li's voice was deep and silky smooth, and left Wong cold inside.

'But Sir! My recommendation was to destroy

the camp in a bombardment. Scorched earth, no survivors.'

Li waved his hand.

'No, this is not possible. The general wishes to be present at their execution. That means you will attack the camp by stealth and bring back the boy and the girl. I don't care what happens to the rest, but you will do this one thing.'

Wong felt like the noose around his neck had just tightened.

'Yes Sir.'

'Excellent. I want your plans for the attack within the hour. Don't fail me Wong.'

'No Sir.'

Back in his office, Wong, still feeling sick to his stomach, drew up the plans for a land attack on the rebel encampment. He was relieved he hadn't killed the mole in camp after the failure of the ambush at the fueling facility.

The day before, at their designated meeting, he had his liaison tell the boy an attack was imminent, and he would be spared only if he took a transponder into camp after months of pleading ignorance of the geography and muddying the waters about the exact location.

It was a lie, of course. He would personally put a bullet in the child's head.

***

Jack sat cross-legged on his bedroll, not yet tired

enough to sleep. His talk with Jen had been unproductive. She denied she was depressed, but at least promised to talk to him if she was feeling down. Before he departed, he asked her if she had any ideas about who might be the mole in camp.

'I have no idea,' she said. 'Everyone is so nice. I don't know if it's even true there is a mole or a rat or whatever you want to call them.'

That was Jen, always seeing the best in people.

That single question stirred in his mind. Kept him awake hours after he put his head on his pillow but ironically, it wasn't until he began to drift off, that a familiar face floated into his mind.

Jack's eyes snapped open.

Todd.

It wasn't just embarrassment on his face earlier. It was guilt.

Chapter 20

Jack woke up early and lay in his bedroll, weighing up how to handle the Todd thing. A little part of him, the part seething with righteous anger, wanted to confront him immediately, knife in hand.

The calmer part of him reasoned that he couldn't be certain of Todd's guilt. At least not until he'd looked him in the eye and asked him the question.

Calm Jack won out and he decided to take his time and sit down to breakfast with everyone before he found Todd and attempted to confirm his suspicions.

Todd was at breakfast when Jack arrived. He was sitting in a far corner, all alone just like an unpopular kid at high school. Jack watched him from the corner of his eye as Murphy ladled oatmeal into his bowl.

'Cheers, Murph,' he said distractedly.

'Everything okay?'

Jack looked at her intelligent eyes.

'Yeah, fine. Bad night's sleep is all.'

'You're not the only one,' she said, nodding past him.

Jack looked around and saw Jen looking dejected as she half-heartedly spooned oatmeal into her mouth.

He winked at Murphy.

'I'm on it.'

'Hey kiddo, want some company?' he asked Jen.

'Sure,' she said, smiling politely.

'How did you sleep?' he asked, glancing across at Todd as he ate.

'Okay, I guess, you?'

That small talk went on for a few minutes, Jen quiet and Jack distracted by the Todd situation. He'd only eaten half his oats when Todd got up and left, looking surreptitiously to his left and right before exiting the tent.

Jack wolfed down the last of his breakfast then looked at Jen.

'Want to go for a walk later? Maybe out to the lake?'

'That'd be nice, but I don't think Hailey wants people going past the perimeter with all the booby traps.'

'Oh yeah, I forgot. Wait, I've got a better idea, how about a game of chess?'

Jack knew she and her cousin Robert used to have a great rivalry when it came to chess, and the happiest he'd ever seen Jen was when the two of them were bickering over who was the best.

The suggestion seemed to perk her up a little and she smiled the first genuine smile he'd seen her give in days.

'Okay,' she said. 'But I'm not going to take it easy on you...'

He laughed.

'You better not!' he said, standing up. 'I'll come find you at 7pm.'

Jack walked to the sleeping tents but found no trace of Todd in or near his tent. Further investigation of the other common areas was fruitless too. On a hunch, he decided to walk the perimeter.

He'd traversed three quarters of the way around, careful of the traps and pitfalls, and was on the western side when he heard a rustling to his right. Jack froze and crouched behind a brush.

Barely five seconds later, Todd emerged, stepping warily over a trip line.

'Todd!' Jack called out and stepped in front of the smaller boy, who flinched and made to run.

Jack grabbed his upper arm and pulled him back to face him.

'J-Jack! What are you doing? Why're you—'

'Quiet Todd. What are you doing out here? You know none of us are supposed to go past the tree line.'

'I – I – I was talking to—'

'Your mom? Sorry Todd, I'm not buying that story anymore.'

Todd shook his hand off.

'Well, what's it to you? Bradley was right. You always leave camp. Who knows what you're friggin' up to, dude.'

Jack took a step backwards to open the space

between them and let his hands hang loosely by his side. From their hand-to-hand training, he knew Todd could fight when he was desperate, so Jack intended to hit him hard and fast if it came to that.

He grinned mirthlessly.

'You know Grandpa has me fixing up old Betsy,'

'What about before that?'

He shook his head.

'Not playing this game, Todd. Just come clean, and we can talk about it.'

'The whole camp knows you're the rat, Jack!' Todd yelled, taking a step backwards, then another.

'Don't move, Todd. Let's just... *SHIT!*'

The smaller kid took off, jumping the tripwire and sprinting into the undergrowth. Jack followed, hot on his heels, pumping his arms and legs as hard as he could, knowing he had to get him before he got clear of the thick undergrowth. Taller and faster, Jack caught up to him in a few strides and tackled the kid hard into the ground on the edge of one of Hailey's pits.

'God damn it,' Jack panted, flipping the kid onto his back. 'You could have killed both of us.'

Todd burst into tears.

'I-I'm s-s-sorry, Jack. I'm s-s-so sorryyyy.'

Jack got up and hoisted him to his feet by the lapels of his jacket and pushed him back against one of the trees.

'Talk.'

The kid just blubbered and shook his head.

Jack wasn't in the mood for playing around and slapped Todd in the face with an open hand.

It had the desired effect. Todd stopped crying, a look of shock on his face.

'Talk, Todd.'

'They… they promised me! They promised me we would be safe, as long as I… as long as I...'

'Promised you what?! What did those fuckers promise you, Todd, I swear to God...'

Now the betrayal was confirmed, Jack's rage began bubbling and boiling to the surface, hotter than ever. He pictured Robert's dead face, thought of Theo sacrificing himself to save Jessie and all the chaos and misery the treachery had brought down upon them.

Then he saw Todd in front of him, weak and defenseless. All he had to do was place his hands around the kid's skinny neck and squeeze…

'They said we would be safe! That no one would die. I just had to show my loyalty… I… I had to tell them about Cold Springs and… and the Operation. Operation Underdog.'

Jack went cold. There it was. The betrayal. The Chinese had planted Todd. Used their kindness and inclusivity and had him sell out Grandpa and Hailey and everyone else in the camp in exchange for the false promise of their safety.

'They made me bring this back to camp.

He pulled a small black object out of his pants pocket and held it out in his hand. There was no mistaking what it was. A transponder.

'Oh, you stupid, stupid kid,' Jack spat. He grabbed the device, dropped it to the ground and proceeded to stomp it to pieces with the heel of his boot. 'You just signed all of our death warrants. When are they coming?'

'I don't know exactly, but it's sometime today or tomorrow.'

Jack let go of Todd's jacket and placed his hands around his neck as the rage burned.

'No!' Todd sobbed. 'Please Jack, they promised! We'll be safe.'

Jack tensed, letting his hands squeeze. Todd began to choke, big fat tears crawling from his eyes and down his cheeks. Jack closed his eyes and relaxed his grip. No matter what the kid had done, he didn't have it in him to kill him in cold blood.

'You're done here, understand? If you want to live, you're going to turn around in the clothes on your back and walk away and keep walking. You can't come back,' Jack finally said. 'If you do, you'll be executed. The camp will riot once they find out it was you and Hailey and Grandpa can't contain that. Not now.'

'But where will I go?' Todd whined, rubbing his throat.

'I don't care Todd. But I wouldn't run to your Chinese buddies, they'll kill you as soon as they find out you're of no further use.'

'But-'

'*Go Todd!*' Jack said, pushing the kid, who fell to

the forest floor. 'If I see you again, I'll finish what I started.'

Todd looked up, face muddied and tear stained.

'Goodbye Todd.'

The kid rolled onto his knees and climbed laboriously to his feet. He looked at Jack one more time before turning and heading deeper into the undergrowth.

Jack waited a few minutes to make sure he didn't come back, then turned and broke into a run heading back into camp.

Once back within the perimeter, he found the camp strangely empty. Where was everybody?

He stopped and looked around, then heard raised voices from the direction of the mess tent. It was too early for dinner, but the tent also doubled as a pseudo town hall... something was up.

Jack sprinted to the tent just in time to see Grandpa stepping down from Chair Rock.

Jack was pushing through the campmates milling around at the edge of the tent, unable to make out the hushed conversations, when a hand grabbed him.

He swung around. It was Bradley.

Jack tensed, ready to punch him in the face, when he said something that surprised him.

'I'm sorry Jack. I really am—I was sure it was you...'

'Huh?'

'Grandpa and Hailey just told us who the mole is.

Look, I was just worried for the camp. You get it, right?'

Jack shook him off and made his way to where Grandpa and Hailey stood in low conversation with Murphy and Ade.

'... find him and bring him to my tent, okay?' Grandpa was saying. 'Jack, where have you been? We know who—'

'Me too Sir, but we don't have time to—'

A small explosion, like the blast of a shotgun in the distance on the eastern side of camp, interrupted him.

'That was one of the tripwires,' said Hailey. 'They're here!'

Chapter 21

'Stations! Now!'

Grandpa's roar of command jolted everyone into action. Jack was moving before most, taking a shortcut by sprinting out of the mess tent and vaulting one of the trenches as he rushed to the weapons tent.

Hailey was there a split second after him and they began to throw every variety of assault rifle they had on the rack onto the long table.

'Grab one and take your designated position!' called Hailey, as their camp mates, headed by Murphy, began to arrive. There was no time to be picky about weapons, they just had to grab what was at hand and get going.

'You and Murphy take a rifle and go, Jack! We need experienced people in those front positions.'

'Okay,' said Jack grabbing an Armalite AR-10 A2, and stuffing two spare magazines into his pockets. 'See you on the other side!'

Murphy ran with him.

'Jack. Where is Todd?'

'Not now. Let's—'

'Where, Jack? Where the hell is he?'

Murphy kept pace with him, her own assault rifle held tight to her chest, waiting for an answer. He couldn't lie, either. Not to her.

'He admitted everything… I let him go Murph,' he said finally.

'I'd have done the same.'

Jack looked at her briefly, before gunfire in the distance caught their attention, prompting them to dive behind a fallen tree.

'You would have?'

'Yup.'

Murphy shot off a burst of fire as Jack stared intently at the shadows between the trees.

'Right, Murph, stay here with the others and keep them from advancing.'

'Where are you going?' she asked, but Jack was already gone, headed back in the direction of camp, leaving Murphy and the armed survivors that had been following on their heels.

Threading his way back through the parade of wide-eyed, alert survivors, all moving to man their designated stations, Jack had a plan.

Recalling how he'd sniped the soldiers who had been attacking Katie, he didn't see why the same tactic, which had come naturally to him with his competition shooting experience, wouldn't work again.

Tucking the gun close to him, he turned northwest before he reached the camp, heading deeper into the trees, knowing the Chinese had been approaching from a southeasterly direction.

With legs pumping and heart racing, Jack ran a good quarter mile through the thick forest before turning a sharp right and beginning to wind his way around to flank the assaulting forces.

The sporadic fire in the distance, mainly coming from the camp defenders, told him that the enemy were moving into place before they began an all-out assault.

Jack slowed to a steady walk when he judged he was within 300 yards of their flank and ducked low, thankful that he'd chosen his khaki pants and green t-shirt to wear that morning. When he spied movement in the distance, he got down on his belly in the mud and leaves and shuffled forward until he was behind a large rock. He took a deep breath to steady himself then drew the rifle up to his shoulder, placing it on a crease in the rock and peering through the iron sight.

It took his eyes a moment to become accustomed to the dappled light, but soon he was able to count off the half-dozen or so soldiers moving stealthily through the shadows in between trees.

It was a small band, perhaps a lead unit sent in to test or report on the camp's defenses. Either way, they were within range and moving closer to his people. He forced himself to relax, taking a deep breath before slowly exhaling until his lungs were empty. That's when he squeezed the trigger.

His target's neck snapped horrifically, blood spurting against the bark of a tree beside him. Jack swiveled his barrel to the right and took the man behind him as the crack of his first shot reached them, revealing they were under fire.

The second man dropped as the rest scattered, and he braced for the return fire. It came, but it was panicked and reactionary, and—aside from a bullet whizzing over his head—nowhere near him.

Thanks to the bowl-like acoustics of the shallow vale they were in, the soldiers had no idea what direction he had fired from. Jack scanned left and right even as a voice called out what he assumed was *ceasefire* in Mandarin.

His aim fell upon a man who, comically, was hiding behind a tree but on the wrong side, giving Jack a full view of his back. This was war and Jack had no qualms about etiquette. He squeezed the trigger and caught the unsuspecting soldier dead-center in the spine.

This time the return fire was heavier and more on target, and Jack was forced to duck down behind the rock cradling his rifle as chips of rock and shredded foliage fell upon him.

Again came the ceasefire call and the assault stopped. Jack remained where he was, aware that they could be waiting for him to pop his head up so they could take it off. That's when he heard the snap of a twig in the distance to his right. They were flanking him, just like he'd done to them.

Jack quickly scrambled around the boulder, putting it between him and the direction of the sound. Peering around the edge, his belly in the grass, he aimed towards the thicket of trees and waited. He didn't have to wait long before spying movement. He switched his weapon to full auto;

sniping was not an option with the enemy this close and hidden by the underbrush.

Three seconds later, a soldier materialized, a second following close behind. Jack fired a burst, rewarded immediately by a blood-curdling scream as the first soldier tumbled forward, holding his belly. He squeezed again, this time taking the solider in the face as shots rang out from his comrade. They whizzed over Jack's hiding place, and he squeezed off a longer burst in the direction the fire had come from, sweeping right to left. He heard a grunt of pain and the shooting ceased.

There was a yell of Mandarin from Jack's left, closer now, no more than 30 yards, and more answers from behind. The six had been reinforced. Five kills would have to do for now. Scrambling back around the rock on hands and knees, he slung the rifle over his back and crawled back to the thicker part of the forest before gaining his feet and running to circle back to Murphy's position. Noting the heavy gunfire that had broken our closer to camp, he reloaded his rifle as he went.

He slowed to a stop as he neared camp from the north, trying to make out how the battle was progressing. It was impossible to tell. The occasional scream told him that some of Hailey's traps were being sprung, but those would only slow the attack, not end it. He was about to run again, when he heard a whoosh in the distance followed immediately by screams of agony and calls of *RUN!*

Jack diverted from the path and climbed a small hill that gave a slightly elevated view of the vale. What he saw was like a punch to the gut. A fire had broken out. He watched an enormous tongue of flame shoot a hundred feet towards the camp, lighting up more trees and eliciting more agonized screams.

Jack saw his campmates running back towards camp and in every other direction, for that matter. Chaos reigned. One familiar figure tried to rally them though—it was Murphy, and she was heading a group of five who were making their way to the northeastern corner of the camp.

He briefly wondered how Grandpa, Hailey and the others were faring at their various positions before setting off at a run to meet Murphy. On lower ground, he lost sight of Murphy and the kids she was leading, but stayed true to the course he'd been following which would eventually cross her path.

It came upon him faster than anticipated and he nearly barreled headlong into her, putting his hands up quickly when she swung her weapon towards him.

'Don't shoot! It's me.'

Murphy pulled up and looked to the sky before bending over with a hand on her knee as she caught her breath.

'What's happening?'

'Nothing,' Murphy said. 'Follow me. They broke through our line with their flamethrowers, and more are coming from the south.'

'More?'

She nodded. 'Jessie got to the water tower and managed to patch through to Grandpa. More are coming. Way more. We need to gat back into camp and regroup.'

'Let's go!'

Murphy and Jack took off, racing back the short distance to the inner perimeter, which was marked by the covered pits with stakes.

'Be careful through here,' Murphy said to their small group.

'Hopefully the enemy throw caution to the wind after seeing the retreat and a few get skewered,' muttered Jack.

The fighting hadn't begun long ago, but Camp Lisa was bleak.

Injured kids were sitting and lying on the ground behind the barricades they'd set up around the inner circle of the camp. Jessie and Jen were moving amongst them, administering aid where they could. Jack looked down in shock when he saw the shapes of three bodies covered with a large blanket near the entrance to the mess tent. A small, blackened foot protruded from under one corner, and he promptly bent over and vomited onto the ground.

The excitement he'd felt when the alarm was raised and then during his own foray had now switched to devastation and clarity upon seeing the results of the combat.

In the end, they were just a bunch of kids against a highly trained army. If they'd stopped to think about it more logically at the beginning, they'd have seen that all their preparation was going to count for nothing when the real fighting began.

Gunfire from the east and south was getting louder now, and more camp survivors were streaming in with every second that passed. There was an explosion somewhere to the east, and smoke from the fires set by the Chinese was starting to creep into camp.

Rustling in the trees on the southern perimeter elicited shouts of horror and Jack quickly raised his rifle as Hailey and Ade burst into view and, ignoring his raised weapon, made a beeline for him. Hailey's smudged face was etched with worry, but she seemed unaware there was a bleeding gunshot wound in her left bicep.

'You've been shot,' Jack said as he lowered his weapon.

Hailey looked down at her wound then back up and around the camp.

'Never mind that now. We need to evacuate.'

Murphy and Jack swapped looks.

'But we're...'

Hailey shook her head.

'No! We need to hold off the worst of them and get these kids into the truck.'

Jack's head spun. It was all coming undone so quickly. How would they fit everyone into the truck? Where would they go? Before he could even seek an answer to his unspoken questions, gunfire erupted from the tree line as Chinese soldiers breached the perimeter.

Chapter 22

Jack felt a sharp sting on his right shoulder and ducked down behind a barricade. Safe for now, he raised his shoulder and looked, relieved to find the wound was only a shallow furrow, left by a round that had skimmed him.

'Are you okay?' asked Murphy.

'Yeah, only nipped me.'

Murphy acknowledged him by firing over the barricade.

'Maybe you wouldn't mind joining in then?'

Ade was beside her, but Hailey had vanished from sight, and he could only hope she'd been able to take cover too. He turned his head just in time to see a kid who was crouching behind a chair a few feet in front of him take a bullet straight to the head before he collapsed, lifeless. Jack felt his stomach flip again before slumping back down under the barricade where Murphy was reloading.

He shook his head.

'There's too many...'

An agonized scream rang out from the direction of the soldiers followed by more frantic Mandarin.

'That is one skewered,' Murphy offered. 'And readied to fire again.'

'No,' Jack said, putting his hand on the warm barrel. 'You heard Hailey. There's too many.'

'Well, until I'm told otherwise...'

She began to rise, her gun at the ready, when the whizz of gunfire over their heads and into the top of the barrier caused her to drop back down just as quickly.

'Shit!'

'Yeah,' he said. 'We... we need to buy the others time, or no one is getting out.'

The words tasted like ashes in his mouth. But it was true. He knew it. Murphy knew it. This wasn't some fairytale where everyone would make it out. This was reality. Cruel and harsh. And if anyone was going to live, some of them would have to fight and lay their lives on the line to make that happen.

'Okay,' she said, and they bumped fists.

'Ade, you find Hailey and lead the survivors out to the truck, we'll lay down suppressing fire.'

He looked like he was going to argue, but then with a sharp nod he got up, crouching low, and started calling the other survivors to him.

'Go!' they both yelled to the kids who were frozen in place, too frightened of being shot to risk moving.

Hailey reappeared from deeper in the camp.

'Come on everybody!' she called, understanding immediately what Jack and Murphy were doing. She threw three magazines across to them. 'Give us five minutes then make your way to the truck!'

Jack gave her the thumbs up with a rueful smile on his face, then turned and began firing with Murphy.

'Just us now,' he said, when he paused to reload.

Murphy grunted and continued to fire before calling 'reloading,' and Jack took over. They worked in tandem like that for a few more minutes before they paused and Jack sat back down with his back against the barricade.

'I have about half a magazine left, if we're going to follow, we need to do it now while we still have ammo.'

'Okay,' said Murphy, 'I have three quarter of my last one left. How are we doing this?'

'You go, I'll follow backwards and lay down fire. When I'm out we'll swap.'

'Let's do it!'

Murphy rose and charged the way the others had gone. Jack jumped up and followed, shooting blindly behind him, hoping it was enough to occupy them and praying a shot wouldn't punch his ticket before they reached the next barricade.

They made it.

'I'm out,' Jack panted.

'Okay. My turn.'

With heads low, the pair ran on, this time Jack leading the way while Murphy methodically laid down suppressing fire. They made it to the tents and out of sight of the enemy, finally, sprinting as hard as they could.

Emerging from the tents on the other side, Jack skidded to a halt. Murphy bumped into him, nearly falling to the ground.

Three dead Chinese, these ones all dressed in

black, lay bleeding on the grass. One's head had been crushed by a rock, another one shot and the last with a cut across his throat deep enough that Jack could see the bone of his spinal column gleaming in the mess.

Near them, a blood-drenched Ade sat with his back against a tree stump with a long hunting knife gleaming crimson in his ham-sized fist. There was a dark, bloody patch on his belly.

'Shit,' Jack said, kneeling beside him. 'You okay?'

A grunt.

'Better than them.'

'Goddamn, Ade!' Said Murphy. 'Come on, we'll get you to the truck.'

Together they managed to take most of Ade's weight and lead him along the narrow path towards the truck. When they got there, Hailey was marshalling the last of the kids onto the first truck. It was already overcrowded. Behind it, the smaller truck, the one that had carried the team to the fuel facility, was almost full.

When she was satisfied that they had as many of the survivors loaded on as possible, Hailey stepped up to Jessie and handed her the keys.

'Go. Take the first truck, get out to the main road, follow it north to the highway, then out around the lake and north. Keep going.'

Jessie frowned.

'You sure?'

'Yes,' Hailey said, glancing over her shoulder as Jack and Murphy arrived with Ade between them.

'Fuck… go, Jessie. We'll be a few minutes behind you in the second truck. Go!'

***

Colonel Jang Li arrived at the chopper and was greeted by Wong, who saluted him then signaled the pilot with a whirl of his finger. The engine began to whine as Li brushed past Wong and climbed aboard.

Once they were strapped in, the helicopter began to rise.

'Progress?' snapped Li.

'Positive, Sir. The two platoons have engaged from the east and south and are driving inward.'

'Casualties?'

'Light, as we expected, Sir.'

'And you have ensured the persons of interest will be captured alive?'

Wong wrung his hands.

'Those orders have been given, Sir… but of course, in the heat of battle—'

'No excuses, Wong! They better be captured alive, or you'll be joining them in the ground.'

'Yes Sir.'

'How long?'

Wong checked his watch.

'Ten minutes approximately, Sir.'

They fell into silence, both lost in thought. Wong nervous, but hopeful that this operation would bring him the promotion he'd so desperately craved for three years. Li, excited to finally deliver the General the killers of his daughter, bringing the months-long mission to a close.

***

Hailey slammed the truck door shut, peering into the flatbed at the 16 pairs of frightened eyes looking back at her from dirty, bloodied faces— hands gripping handguns, rifles, or anything they had grabbed in their hurry.

Under their feet were a few bags of supplies containing bare essentials that had been thrown in at the last minute. This was it. Travel light and get the hell out of dodge.

Jessie leaned out the window, hands extended, which Hailey gripped hard, and stepped forward to embrace her.

'You've got this, girl,' Hailey said.

'I'm...' Jessie stopped, fighting the urge to fall into a pit of self-doubt as the sound of gunfire continued in the background, punctuated by a scream. It seemed to focus her. 'I'll see you soon.'

Jessie settled into the driver's seat and hollered to the kids in the back to hold on tight. A second later, the truck tore off down the dirt track, heading northwest for the roads out of the forest.

'God speed, kids,' whispered Hailey.

A burst of static came from the walkie talkie on her belt and she raised it as Murphy and Jack began to tend to Ade. They were using a first aid kit they had found in the pile of supplies that didn't fit onto the truck.

'That you, old timer?'

Only static.

'Hey, Dad. You read me, over?'

Nothing.

She swore and tucked it back into her belt, knowing she didn't have the luxury of time to keep trying the comms. She turned back to the others, where Murphy was wrapping a wide bandage around Ade's midriff as Jack held him upright.

'That's it,' said Hailey. 'Make it tight and go around three or four times. Have we got everyone?'

'Bradley's back in the middle of camp,' said Murphy. 'He mumbled something about a surprise for them.'

The words were barely out of her mouth when Bradley came running into the clearing. Behind him, a pall of smoke—much blacker than the smoke from the fires the Chinese had set—began rising into the sky.

'Gasoline!' he blurted as he pulled to a skidding halt in front of them. 'I poured two barrels into the trenches and lit it up. No way are they getting past that in a hurry. The others, they got out?'

'Yeah, Jessie's gone. It's just us now, so time to go. Everyone to the truck. Ade, you ride up front with me.'

The ashen-faced Ade didn't argue, but he was strong enough to gently extricate himself from Jack's arms.

'I'm okay to walk.'

'Good,' said Hailey. 'Let's go!'

Chapter 23

Jessie's hands gripped the truck's steering wheel like the reigns of a wild stallion as the vehicle lurched and bucked along the dirt track. Her speed and the poor condition of the road threatened to crash them headlong into the trees on more than a few occasions.

Suddenly from behind her, over the roar of the engine, she heard shouts and screams that were different to those elicited by the wild ride.

'Everything alright back there!?'

Her breath stuck in her throat as she focused on the track's winding path, the speedometer creeping up to 60mph.

'They've got bikes!'

'What!?'

'MOTORBIKES!'

On cue, she spotted a soldier in full uniform bent low over the handlebars of a motocross bike, zipping through the woods to their right. He disappeared briefly, and she yelled to Ruby who was riding shotgun, 'Where did he go?! Can you see him?!'

Ruby didn't have a chance to answer when the bike reappeared from the trees next to them and sped past, veering onto the road in front of them.

'Shit!' Jessie yelled, twitching the wheel,

whipping the truck to the left and slowing down.

This seemed to play right into the soldier's hands, and he leaned over, pulling an object that Jessie realized quickly was a machine pistol, from a fixed holster and aimed it behind him.

He let off a volley of bullets, which pinged into the front of the truck. Without thinking, Jessie slammed her foot down on the gas and swerved left to avoid the gunfire. The rider adjusted and let off another burst that stitched along the hood of the truck, one round piercing the windshield right between her and Ruby.

'That's it, fucker!' yelled Jessie and zeroed on the rider.

Apparently confident he could kill her before she hit him, he let off another burst of fire which went awry when his front tire struck a rock. He managed to keep his balance, but Jessie had now closed the gap and the bulbar kissed the back of the soldier's bike. The bike flipped backwards, both it and the rider striking the windshield and clattering away either side of the speeding vehicle.

'Holy shit!' Ruby cried. 'You got him good!'

But it wasn't over. From behind, the roar of more bikes.

'You packing?' Jessie called to Ruby, as she weaved the truck through the last of the dirt track, and skidded into a half-spin as she turned onto the asphalt of the road leading out northwest from the park.

In answer, Ruby pulled a 12-gauge shotgun from

her right side, much to Jessie's surprise.

'Yep!'

Jessie smirked.

'Nice. Can you shoot it, is the question?' She checked the mirrors, watching as one of the kids pulled a handgun up from the flatbed and fired at the soldiers behind them. To her pleasure, the kid—Jared—who was only 14, managed to get a headshot and one of the bikes veered off the road and straight into a tree.

The surviving pursuer fired back, and Jessie saw Jared fall backwards as the bike crossed into the other lane and sped up the right hand side of the truck.

'Quick, Ruby! He's coming up on your side.'

Ruby nodded, her jaw set and red hair streaming in the wind as she moved off the seat, rested one knee on it then pumped the shotgun, aiming it through the window but careful to keep the barrel out of sight.

The bike tore up their flank and when he was level with the passenger side door, Ruby squeezed the trigger.

The shot was loud in the enclosed space and the sheer force of the recoil sent her tiny frame slamming into Jessie. After she got the wheel back under control, Jessie looked in the mirrors to see the crumpled form of the soldier and, a few feet away, his steaming motorbike.

Jessie let out a long sigh and looked at Ruby, who was back in her seat, staring down at the shotgun in disbelief.

'Did I…?'

'Yeah, he's down, good work Ruby.'

Ruby looked over her shoulder and much to her relief saw Jared sitting up and looking back at her. He was holding his shoulder but gave her a thumbs up.

She couldn't see any more bikes and there was no sign of Hailey in the second truck. She slowed as the road they were on came to a junction and turned right.

'This should take us to the highway,' Jessie said, finally relaxing as the adrenaline in her system began to dissipate. The air breezing through the windows was refreshing, and everyone was still alive and in one piece in the flatbed. She allowed a sense of optimism to wash over.

It receded quickly when they rounded a bend and saw in the distance, across all lanes of the highway, a line of green-painted vehicles with flashing lights and soldiers running this way and that, putting the finishing touches on a roadblock.

**

Jack and Murphy were the last onto the back of the truck; he slapped the side of the vehicle and screamed for Hailey to go.

She didn't need telling twice and Jack almost lost his seat as the truck took off and made quick work of the winding track that would take them out from the deep of the forest. Once they made the paved road, Jack took the time to look back. The horizon was black with smoke, and he spotted several helicopters hovering over the spot they had just fled.

'That was a good move with the gasoline,' he said to Bradley.

His nemesis of the last few days nodded and smiled.

'I figured we wouldn't be needing it,' said the other kid, then his expression changed, and he pointed at the road ahead. 'Is that…?'

It was a mangled body at the side of the road. There was debris all over the road and as Hailey slowed to weave through and around it they saw the wrecked bike in the long grass on the other side.

'It's a Chinese soldier. They must have been waiting on the road,' said Murphy.

Jack strained to look further up the road. Sure enough, they were almost past it when he saw more wreckage and another crumpled body at the foot of a tree well off the side of the road.

'Looks like Jessie outmaneuvered them,' said Bradley.

Jack didn't comment. He was too tense, knowing the possibility they would round a bend and find the truck in a wreck, or worse, was high.

'Damn. Another one!' called Murphy.

Jack let out a breath and looked over the side as they passed another corpse, this one missing most of its face courtesy of a shotgun blast. Whoops of joy went up from the other kids in the truck.

He didn't join in. His nerves were on edge, suddenly anxious how easy their escape had seemed. Sure, the firefight in the forest had been intense and they'd lost a lot of people, but it didn't seem quite right. Why hadn't the Chinese just obliterated them with artillery? Once they had their location it would have been easy enough.

Jack scrambled back through the flatbed, nodding and apologizing to his friends as he squeezed up to the truck's cabin. There, he tapped on the glass window, which Ade slid open. He put his head in and asked, 'Hey, has Grandpa touched base?'

'No,' Hailey replied, then added optimistically, 'Not yet.'

'Right.'

'Why?'

'This seems too easy. Why didn't they just bomb the camp?'

'I was contemplating the same question myself,' Hailey said.

'Should we stop? What if we're heading into a trap?'

'We can't stop, Jack. What purpose would it serve? Look, just keep everyone hunkered down back there. We're almost to the highway.'

Jack nodded. She was right of course. What would they do if they stopped? Hide? They were already in a trap and the jaws were closing. He shared a look with Murphy as he squeezed past her, one that filled him with a warmth that was alien to the situation they were in. What was that?

He sat back down between Bradley and Jen, and they searched his face for clues to what he'd been discussing.

'We keep an eye out, and hunker down if it gets rough,' he said. 'We're almost free—'

His voice was cut off as Jen raised her hand.

'Do you hear that?' she said.

'Hear what?'

'That.'

One of the younger kids in the truck with them, a girl called Sofia, cocked her head. 'I think it's a helicopter...'

***

There they were. Like ants on the floor, ready to be squashed, Li thought as he watched the truck below them.

The pilot maneuvered expertly over the road, winding its way through the forest high to track the truck but also to get a good look ahead.

Sure enough, in the distance Jang Li could make out the highway blockade that had been set up in place, on orders followed by Wong.

'Well done,' Jang Li conceded. 'You've done well. I can see they've already had casualties.'

Pointing at a position about 300 yards short of the roadblock, fire and smoke belched up from an overturned truck, the area around it lit up with sparks of gunfire. No doubt, the soldiers engaging with the rebels who had survived the crash.

Not for long, he thought.

Below, and oblivious to the fate of their comrades, Jang Li watched the truck following the same route to the blockade.

But he wasn't here to be passive, and he wouldn't fail this time—not like Huntsville. Bending over, he pulled a heavy green box out from under the seat.

Wong looked at him curiously.

'I reconsidered my position. You were right when you said anything can happen in the heat of battle. Do you agree, Wong?'

'Yes Colonel, I understand completely.'

Pulling out the Light Machine Gun with great care, he positioned it on a mounted stand at the edge of the helicopter's open door and secured it in place with the help of Wong, then stood aside as his subordinate loaded it.

'Stand aside, Wong,' he smiled thinly. 'I deserve this, don't you think? Pilot, take us in closer, over.'

'Roger, Colonel. Going in.'

The helicopter's rapid descent gave Jang Li's stomach a jolt, but it was a pleasurable one. It excited him and the thrill of the hunt consumed him. Gripping the LMG, he swiveled it on its stand, and aimed at the truck as they descended rapidly.

⁕

'Hailey! FLOOR IT!' Jack screamed as he pushed those around him down onto the bed of the truck. The helicopter swept over their position, unleashing a hell-like storm of high caliber bullets that punctured the road behind them as the gun's operator zeroed in on them.

Hailey swerved left and right over the road, tires squealing, sending kids bucking and flying about in the back, hanging on for dear life.

Jack, buried by the limbs of his comrades, locked eyes with Jen. Hers were filled with fear, but not panicked; they'd been through similar danger in the past and survived, and he hoped they'd look back and laugh at this some time.

Hailey was doing a good job of veering out of the line of fire, but the chopper pilot was onto her and banked right so that the gunner on his left would have a better and uninterrupted line of sight.

'Hold on tight!' Hailey screamed and swung the truck off the road. It was a last-ditch effort to avoid the chopper by getting under the trees, but Jack knew it was almost certainly hopeless.

The mechanical, staccato noise of the machine gun continued above them as of the truck careened towards the trees. Jack saw a decent-sized gap between two trees and knew that's what Hailey was aiming for.

He was about to yell hold on again when suddenly the truck nose dived into a ditch that had been hidden by long grass. Jack tried to brace, but the force of the impact as it hit the ground threw him forward and over the top of the cabin.

Jack lay on the grass looking into the impossibly

blue sky, wondering if he was dead. The noise of the helicopter and groaning around him told him instantly he was not. Dazed and dizzy, he lurched to his feet and looked around. Everything sounded distorted and he felt sick in the stomach.

The chopper was less than 300 yards away, about 200 yards high, and it looked like the operator of the gun was trying to reload it. Gunfire further down the road drew his attention and he saw the wreck of the first truck and realized Jessie and the others were under heavy fire.

Behind them, the helicopter whined, and Jack turned again as the pilot descended to just 40 feet above the road, its blades whipping up dust and grass as the large machine gun muzzle turned in their direction.

'Run to Jessie!' called Hailey, her voice cutting through the fog in his head. 'We'll make our last stand there!'

He went to take a step, but something soft bumped his foot and almost caused him to trip. When he looked down, he saw little Sofia, her head twisted at an acute angle, blue eyes staring sightlessly into the same sky he'd been looking at a few seconds before.

'Run Jack!' said Murphy grabbing him by the collar and pulling him.

A deep sob escaped his lips as he allowed himself to be dragged along. So deep was his shock, he didn't hear the sound of hope from the heavens. The roar of Grandpa's Curtiss P-36 Hawk as it descended at speed, its guns suddenly singing their own staccato rata-tat-tat.

Chapter 24

'Howdy, assholes!' said Grandpa through gritted teeth.

His beautiful, shiny, patched-up Betsy cut through the air like a hawk, swooping in low over the adjacent trees and tearing up to the highway from a right angle. The gunfire shredded the roadblock to pieces, sending Chinese soldiers scattering.

Once past, he pulled the joystick back and hard to the left and Betsy gained altitude, banking back towards the road where the second truck had come to a standstill.

He was only sorry it'd taken him so long to get here. He hadn't expected the ambush at the garage, but then the five soldiers they'd sent for him hadn't expected some old coot to be sneaking through the trees with an AK-47 and a 9mm Glock

It had been pretty intense, and without the element of surprise he wouldn't have survived. As it was, nestled tight in the cockpit, his blood-drenched hands struggled to maintain a grip on the joystick. He hadn't escaped unscathed. He'd been hit in the left shoulder and another bullet had left a deep furrow in his side between the rib and hip.

The plane straightened and began to follow the

ribbon of asphalt below, but he only had eyes for the black helicopter that had turned its side to the people running. He put his finger back on the trigger of the guns and was about to squeeze when a hail of bullets from behind struck the tail of the aircraft.

Suddenly Betsy tried to spin to the left, and he knew instantly the stabilizers on the tail had been damaged. It took all of his strength to hold the joystick straight with his good right arm; there was no way he could fire the guns with his nerve-damaged left arm.

Ahead of him the gunner on the chopper opened fire on the survivors running from the second truck.

'Oh well, lets see how you like a serving of hot apple pie, bitches!'

He wasn't going home, but he'd make sure that at least the assholes in the chopper didn't either. He pushed the joystick forward, still wrestling to hold Betsy on an even keel as he dived towards the helicopter.

The pilot and occupants were oblivious to the incoming danger, intent on wiping out the escapees. Grandpa took the opportunity to look down as he sped towards the chopper and saw the figure leading his people stop and look up at Betsy.

It was Hailey. Beautiful, strong Hailey, her dark hair blowing in the wind. A tear fell from his eyes as he lifted his limp left hand in a wave goodbye.

'Goodbye my Baby Girl...'

***

'No! Dad!' Hailey screamed.

Jack and Murphy stopped next to her and watched in awe as the old plane dived towards the chopper.

In the flying machine, Colonel Li saw the leader of the group below pause and look skyward. He ceased firing. *What is she…?*

He leaned forward and followed her gaze. The sight of the old warplane was like a slap in the face.

'Incoming!' He screamed, but by the time the warning had left his lips it was too late. He heard Wong scream behind him.

The last sight that registered in his brain was the grinning face of the old man steering death his way at an impossible speed. Li's world was swallowed then in searing heat and light as the plane torpedoed into the helicopter, engulfing both machines in a blazing ball of fire and sending twisted burning metal to the road top.

***

Jack grabbed both Murphy and Hailey and pushed them to the ground as a wave of heat scorched the air, carrying with it pieces of burning wreckage and debris.

Miraculously, none of them were hurt and when he knew it was safe, he climbed off them and helped them get back up to their feet as they surveyed the damage. Jack could see Hailey was in shock, but the fighting wasn't over. From the blockade, soldiers who had survived Grandpa's strafing were still firing at the survivors of the first truck.

'Come on, we need to get to the others!'

Hailey seemed to come to her senses and the three of them began running again. Jack avoided looking at the broken bodies scattered around them as they joined the survivors behind the overturned truck. Jen and Ade were already there, along with the others who had survived their own truck crash and the subsequent helicopter assault.

Jack gauged the numbers on both sides, and it was clear that Grandpa's aerial intervention has significantly evened the odds. He felt hope begin to burn in his mind, hope that they might find a way out of this after all.

It appeared Hailey had been doing the same calculations.

'We've got to push through,' she mustered finally, and Jack could tell it summoned a lot of guts and energy for her to assert herself.

'Ade, Jessie, Ruby and Jen, I want you to lay down heavy fire with everyone else, while Murphy, Jack, Bradley and I attack from the left.'

Once everyone was across the plan, the cover team began to fire and the four attackers broke cover and, in a crouching run, headed for a wrecked Jeep at the far left end of the barricade.

The cacophony of blazing cover fire from behind them did the trick, and Jack seized the moment to lead the others around the wreckage.

Clearly, the soldiers behind the barricade hadn't expected such a bold move from children and the group of armed campmates took them completely by surprise. A brief firefight ensued, and they killed five soldiers, the last two fleeing into the trees to the left of their position.

Jack whooped and high-fived Murphy before he turned to celebrate with Bradley and Hailey. The happy smile died on his lips when he saw Bradley on his back, with Hailey kneeling over him. Jack saw the hole in his forehead just before Hailey put a handkerchief over his face.

When she stood up, her face was devoid of expression. She took a final look around and then took both Jack and Murphy by the hand.

'Come on, let's go and get the others.'

Compartmentalizing their grief to deal with at a later time, Hailey and the older kids, including Jack, shepherded the survivors, all 14 of them, through to the other side of the barricades. They found two Chinese vehicles still drivable; one looked like the equivalent of a Hummer and the other was a bullet-riddled but miraculously working pick-up truck.

It would be a tight squeeze, but they had enough room for everyone. Under Hailey's guidance they siphoned fuel from other wrecked vehicles and loaded as much ammunition and weaponry as they could carry.

'Jack, are you good to drive the pick-up?' Hailey asked.

'Yep. Any ideas where we should go?'

'Yes, Albany, New York.'

Murphy laughed.

'That's very specific, why Albany?'

'Well Grandpa and I haven't told any of you, but we've been picking up chatter. Apparently, someone launched a counterattack against the Chinese a month ago and they've abandoned the territory east of the Appalachians and Albany has been mentioned a lot. We... I think its worth checking out.'

She was assaulted with questions. *What counterattack? Is it the army? Is the president alive?*

'I can't answer any of those questions!' she called over the top of them. 'I can tell you I don't think it's the army, although I have no idea what could have driven them back if it wasn't. What I can tell you, is it's no use staying here. The camp is gone, and the invaders are in full control of Texas. If anyone has a better idea, shoot.'

No one did, so the decision was made. Albany, New York it was.

Epilogue

'You were right, you know,' Jack remarked as he leaned against the rails of the truck's bed, swigging some water.

Hailey, who took the cannister from Jack to take her own drink, smiled. 'I'm always right. Got raised by the best.'

'That, I can't argue with.'

'Good,' she said. 'But which time are you talking about?'

'This,' he said, gesturing to the city 10 miles distant, which from this position looked like it sprouted from the middle of a forest.

They were on the Helderberg escarpment, overlooking Albany and its surrounds. The view was breathtaking, and the ideal spot to survey what they hoped might become their new home. Their travels had taken longer than anticipated, with the scarcity of fuel and fresh water.

But they'd made it, and word they'd picked up from other groups and travelers they'd met along the way was that a large resistance had dug itself in at Albany.

'Ah,' Hailey replied. 'Well, we're close now. But I'm not taking credit until we get there and find it's what we're looking for.'

Murphy appeared and went over to Jack, slipping her arms around him and looking out.

'The view,' she whispered. 'It's beautiful.'

She wasn't lying. As the late summer sun set across the city, streaks of magenta, red and orange stretched out across the horizon. They drank in the rich display of colors, taking the time to really enjoy their rest. It had been so long since Texas, and they had all seen so much.

Hailey smiled. Jack and Murphy becoming a couple had happened naturally and quickly so that barely any of them noticed. It made her happy— both of them, all of them for that matter, deserved to find what happiness they could in this new harsh world.

It brought her dad to mind, and she suddenly remembered something from her very last conversation with him.

'I have something for you, Jack,' she said.

'You do?'

'Yeah, wait here.'

Hailey went back to the trucks and found the fanny pack she'd carried all the way from Texas with her. She rummaged through the small compartment until she found what she was looking for amongst the assorted items, palming it before heading back to the lookout.

Murphy took her leave when Hailey got back.

'Oh, you don't have to go, it's no big secret,' said Hailey.

'It's fine, I'll go help the others top up the canteen.'

'What's up?' said Jack.

'I have something I was supposed to give you, but I forgot all about it. I should have done it sooner.'

'Oh?' he was genuinely taken aback, and couldn't figure, for the life of him, what it could be. 'I think you have excuses for not remembering.'

Hailey smiled.

'Yeah, well here it is,' she said and held out her hand.

Laying in her palm was a copper penny. Jack plucked it up and inspected it. It was stamped 1914 and the side profile of Abe Lincoln adorned one side.

'It was my dad's lucky penny,' said Hailey, her voice cracking. 'His dad gave it to him on his death bed. He gave it to me just before the attack and said I should give it to you for helping with Betsy and that he hoped it would bring you as much luck as it had brought him.'

Jack was suddenly overwhelmed with emotion and unsure what to say or do. Hailey spared him the need to do anything by taking him in her arms and hugging him tight.

'Thanks,' he said when they parted, wiping a tear from his eye. 'Grandpa was the best, I miss him.'

Hailey put her arm around his shoulder, and they walked back to the parking lot.

'You and me both, kid. Come on, let's get these everyone packed and head into Albany. I've got a good feeling about this...'

The End.

We hope you enjoyed Texas Fight.

Don't miss Messenger (book 9) and The Drifter (Book 10) out now exclusively on Amazon.

If you're up to date, why not try ***Rabid States*** -Scott's new post apocalyptic epic.

www.scottmedbury.com

Printed in the USA
CPSIA information can be obtained
at www.ICGtesting.com
CBHW051258180824
13368CB00006B/210

9 798848 611281